The Sacrifice

Book One of the Forbidden Kiss Series

By Christy Lynn

The Sacrifice

Christy Lynn

This book is a work of fiction. Any references to historical events, real people or places is used fictitiously. Other names, characters, places, and events are products of the author's imagination. Any resemblance to actual events or persons or places, living or dead, is entirely coincidental.

Copyright © 2019 by Christy Richie.

All rights reserved. International copyright secured.

The Sacrifice

Christy Lynn

ABOUT THE AUTHOR

Being raised in the Appalachian Mountains of rural West Virginia, helped tremendously in forging my imagination. I was first published at the age of ten.

I've always known I wanted to be an author, but life got in the way, and it was twenty-five years before I was able to pick up the pen again. I am completely in love with history, fantasy, and romance; therefore, my genre is historical romance and fantasy.

I enjoy creating story lines that involve extensive research, and making my characters come alive for myself and my readers.

I am currently living in Northwest region of the Great Lakes, where I am now a full time author.

The Sacrifice

Christy Lynn

ALSO BY CHRISTY LYNN

THE WALKER GIRL

She has no knowledge of love, marriage, or motherhood. At just twenty-five, her future as an old maid is set. That is, until she learns an arrangement has been made for her hand in marriage.

In every bargain, there is an exchange: Sage will have a husband, but in return must provide her new family with grandchildren. Innocent in the ways of intimacy, she will have to set her insecurities aside to learn how to please her husband. Can she be the submissive wife he has been searching for?

The Sacrifice

Christy Lynn

PART ONE

The Sacrifice

Christy Lynn

CHAPTER 1

She was hungry. Nearly a month had passed since she last fed, and frankly, the need was becoming unbearable. Why did she do this to herself? Every time she submitted to the guilt of her nature and forbid herself to partake in carnal pleasure, she suffered tremendously for weeks. She always ended up caving in and doing it again anyway; so, what was the point, all this martyrdom? Still, she had to try, had to try to save whomever she could from what she was.

She knew it was ridiculous to revel in isolation, depriving herself of the company of others. But her disposition tended to always lean toward moodiness and depression in times like this, keeping her trapped in a mire of sulkiness. Another century was about to turn…and another person was about to die.

Whose idea was it to sacrifice a human to the Goddess Lilith every one hundred years? Lilith was quite capable of claiming a victim of her own whenever she pleased, she didn't need a coven serving someone up cold, so to speak. Brigid shook her head in disgust; this year she would not participate in taking the life of an innocent human, no matter how offended the Goddess might be.

The Sacrifice

How long had Brigid Whelan sat there staring out the window at the treetops of Central Park? She had no idea, but it was long enough that her right leg, which was folded beneath her, had fallen asleep. She rose from her seat, flexing her calf muscle as the pinpricks began; an annoying pain that sets one's teeth on edge.

Suddenly, she heard the front door open, then softly close. The gentle click of the latch as it fell into place caused her ears to perk up. She didn't bother to look who entered, she already knew. Even though he tiptoed quietly across the smooth, hardwood flooring, it was useless to try to sneak up on her. However, Brigid patronized her guest, waiting patiently, eyes intent on the view.

"HA!" Barrex dug his fingers into Brigid's tender sides, laughing as she jumped. "Gotcha!"

She grinned up at him and rolled her eyes.

"I didn't get you?" he let his bottom lip puff out in an exaggerated pout.

Brigid shook her head. "No, brother, you didn't. You should know by now, you never will."

"Yeah, well, that's what you think." Barrex pirouetted from the window to the leather sofa, dramatically dropping onto the soft cushions. "One of these days, one of these days. So, this is where you've been hiding?" He scanned the room with a bored sweep of his large, brown eyes.

Brigid took the chair opposite the sofa and sipped from a tumbler that had been sweating a

Christy Lynn

ring onto the heavy, wooden coffee table. "I'm not hiding. I live here."

"Which baffles the hell out of me. Why can't you stay at your condo in the Tower? All this gloomy, dark wood...so Van Helsing." He rested his head on his fist. "Ya know, its women like you that create all the stereotypes."

"I resent that," Brigid shot back, suddenly losing all humor. Here she was, trying her best to be a good, law-abiding citizen, trying not to kill people, and her own brother wants to accuse her of being stereotypical! Her greenish-yellow eyes turned icy, narrowing as she began gathering a string of curse words to shout at him. "What is this, Pick on Brigid Day?"

"You might resent the dig, but I resent your taste in interior decorating and...," Barrex made a sweeping gesture with his hand, then flashed an irresistibly sweet smile in his sister's direction to try to soften the insult.

"I don't see how attempting to maintain a level of dignity can be construed as a bad thing, brother." Brigid gathered her long, honey-brown hair in her hand and tossed it off her shoulders, preparing for whatever reason had brought her big brother to her sanctuary. "There's certainly no dignity to be found in that get-up you're wearing. Yellow? It's not a color that suits you."

Barrex's mouth dropped open. He put his hand on his chest and gave her a mock look of

The Sacrifice

horror. "This is Dior, how dare you?"

She sat back and folded her arms across her chest, exhaling a heavy sigh. "What do you want, Barry?"

"What?" he batted his long lashes. "Must I want something in order to visit my lil' sis?" He caught the look of doubt she gave him. "OK, I needed a break. I'm sure you can understand? Anne has the entire Tower in an uproar over this year's centennial celebration. Why this one is any different than all the others, beats me." He hopped up and headed for the kitchen.

"Celebration? Is that what the coven is calling it, now?" Brigid muttered, but her thoughts were already drifting toward the Tower.

The Tower - a beautiful, ultra-modern condominium building on Fifty-Seventh Street; now known as Billionaire's Row. Their coven purchased the entire building before the area became the place to live for the upwardly mobile. The acquisition allowed every member to reside together in safety and seclusion. Each apartment was lavishly decorated in the latest fashion. Bright, sleek appliances and smooth, curvy furniture strategically placed between enormous windows and steel beams. All the latest comforts - at the latest prices.

"Perhaps all the stress over this particular century is the technology. We have never had to worry about our victims being so connected, like

Christy Lynn

they are these days. People are informed in ways that, if we aren't completely careful, could expose us." Brigid took another sip of her water.

Barrex shrugged. "I guess. Yeah, you have a point."

Brigid's nose wrinkled with distaste as Barrex sauntered in from the kitchen with a glass of chardonnay. "What's that look for?" He nestled back into the overstuffed couch.

"Nothing," she mumbled.

His gaze rolled in her direction. "Honestly, Blue, why do you hate the coven so much? We live as we do because we can. Call it a benefit of immortality...money." He grinned, rubbing his forefinger and thumb together in the universal sign of greed. "Don't you remember those we've met who haven't made successful use of their years? They're shameful! Simply, um," he searched for the correct description. "Slimy."

Brigid laughed out loud at the word. "Slimy? Could you sound more gay?"

"Yes, I can. Come on, they're disgusting creatures that make your skin crawl. I mean, jeesh, there's absolutely no excuse to lurk around in dark alleys, or live as legends in swamps." He closed his eyes, as if trying to keep from seeing a scary scene in a horror movie.

"It's bad enough we are what we are, would you have us live like vermin, as well? Tell me you haven't forgotten the years we left Anne, before

The Sacrifice

she formed the coven, and were on our own?" Barrex suddenly appeared shaken, his handsome face turning slightly pale, losing all its animated humor. "Unspeakable times. I wouldn't return to that existence for anything, Blue, I mean it."

"Of course, I haven't forgotten. Don't be ridiculous," Brigid snapped, uncomfortable with the sudden change in conversation and wishing she had not brought it up.

Over the centuries, she'd learned how to suppress memories that would send her into an emotional, downward spiral. Thinking of the things she and Barrex had to do at times to survive; it was enough to make her want to open a window and jump from her apartment on the eighteenth floor. It's a terrible thing trying to exist with millions of people, thinking you are one of them when you're not, and having no idea what you truly are; as they did in the early years.

She was suddenly tired of New York and the temptation to travel once again warmed her belly. Japan is lovely this time of year; the cherry blossoms would be in full bloom, and the festivals..., she thought.

"Blue!" her brother's sharp tone startled her from her thoughts. "Are you listening to me?"

"Not really, I'm sorry. What did you say?"

"I asked what you were thinking when I got here?" His brown eyes stared directly at her. "Don't play stupid. When I came in, you were lost

Christy Lynn

in thought, staring out your window. You always stare out a window when you're really stressed or bothered. So, what is it?"

"Do I?" Brigid grinned, pleased to discover her brother still paid such close attention to her. After centuries together, she certainly wasn't surprised.

Suddenly, his brow creased in concern. He leaned forward, resting his elbows on his knees and craning his neck slightly to peer closer at her, like he was critiquing a painting on exhibit. "My god, Blue, seriously? Not again," he sighed and rubbed his forehead in exasperation. "How long has it been since you had sex?"

She stretched, so bored she could hardly sit still. "Not your business." She laced her fingers together, resting them in her lap. Seeing clearly Barrex was not going to let the topic rest, she frowned at him. "Fine, a few weeks."

Barrex's eyes narrowed. "A few weeks? By the looks of it I'd say more like a month. We are five-hundred-sixty-three years old, get over it!"

Brigid's left brow rose in sudden anger. "Get over it?"

"Yes, Blue, get over it. You think I don't know, but you get like this every time a century turns. For god's sake, why?"

Brigid eyed her brother, trying to suppress the resentment and anger that had been building over the years toward his friendship with the coven. "Please don't tell me that my brother, my own

The Sacrifice

flesh and blood, has no problem watching an innocent human being taken to the penthouse of the Tower to have his life drained, supposedly by the Goddess Lilith, as an offering on our behalf."

"Supposedly?" Barrex questioned.

"Yes, supposedly! Have you ever seen Lilith? Just because Anne says she appears to her every century to claim a human, does not mean she does. Why would Lilith appear only to her, why not the entire coven? Gods and goddesses tend to be rather vain, or so the myths say. So, wouldn't she want a full coven worshipping at her feet?"

Barrex eyed Brigid. "Don't hold back, say how you really feel." He tried to make a joke but opened a can of worms he didn't want opened.

"OK, I will. If you really want to know what has me so pissed perhaps it has something to do with you being such a cozy companion with the woman who killed our mother!"

"Oh, come on, not this again. Anne had no choice, you know that," Barrex snapped. Irritably, he sat back and rubbed his face with both hands, leaving his eyes and cheeks red. "She did what she had to, nothing more. You act as if she plotted Mother's death, or something. I refuse to be lured into this argument for the millionth time. What the fuck, Blue?" he huffed, jumping up from the couch and storming across the room toward the front door. "Bye, darling, I'm off to the museum," he called over his shoulder.

Christy Lynn

Brigid shot him a questioning look. "What? I'm hungry," he stated matter-of-factly. "Not all of us sulk around starving ourselves, Saint Whelan."

"I'm doing it this time. I'm going to let it happen," she said, her tone flat.

Barrex had heard her threaten to commit the only kind of suicide their kind can commit a hundred times before. Over the years, he'd learned how to ignore it. "What has happened to you? Has time made you so weak?" With a defiant jerk of his chin, he whirled around to leave, but paused once more. "I know what you need to break you out of this one-hundred-year funk. I'll pick you up at nine o'clock sharp. You need a night out." Before she could protest, the door slammed behind him.

Brigid settled back into her chair, her brow creased into the well-worn line that sits a little to the left of the bridge of her nose. She returned to her earlier reverie, feeling only slightly guilty she had lied to her brother. She wasn't really thinking of their mother. She'd actually been thinking of both of their parents. How much had they loved each other to endure the process of mating?

She shook her head slowly. Suddenly, she was relieved she had never met another of her kind and fallen in love; there is just no way she could share a man she loved with another, regardless of the reason.

The Sacrifice

***

Brigid knew Barrex well enough to take him seriously, and when he said he would pick her up at nine o'clock sharp, he meant it. She stepped off the elevator at eight-fifty-five; a gray, all-weather trench that came just above her knee concealed her outfit beneath. But it couldn't hide the sheer, black hosiery that covered her shapely legs. She loved this particular style of nylons, with its sexy seam that ran from ankles to buttocks.

She caught the doorman's sweeping gaze that started at chest level and stopped at her black, Christian Louboutin heels. Without a word, she breezed past him, tossing a nonchalant wave in his direction. She refused to look at him for fear she'd rush over and wrap herself around his plump body. She wasn't lying to her brother when she said she'd been cooped up in her apartment for nearly a month, eating human food that could sustain her organic body, but not satisfy the demand of her nature.

Brigid stared out the glass door, watching for Barrex and fidgeting nervously as a feeling all too familiar began building deep inside...hunger. Not hunger as man would know it, but an insatiable arousal that if not satiated through sexual contact, would at first, become unbearably painful then progress to physical symptoms synonymous with the flu.

Christy Lynn

She was a succubus, her brother an incubus; needing to feed from the lifeforce - chi - of humans in order to survive the duration of immortality in good health. Her kind was incapable of producing their own life's energy and therefore had to drain it from the ever-available human population. If a succubus reaches the point of physical reaction to lack of chi, she or he, could easily slip into a coma-like state for eternity – the only suicide a succubus can commit. Brigid played with this perilous 'edge of the envelope' too often; secretly hoping one time she would take it too far and fall into that blissful oblivion that would end her loneliness and ease the guilt that plagued her soul.

At precisely nine o'clock, a large, black Bentley sedan rolled smoothly to a halt at the curb outside, pulling Brigid from thoughts of pushing the poor doorman into the maintenance closet and literally fucking him to death. The standard rule of never eat where you live was, in her current state, becoming steadfastly impossible to obey.

"Have a good evening, Miss Whelan," the doorman's high-pitched, nasally voice reached her.

Without a backward glance, Brigid bolted out the door; the alluring, red bottoms of her stilettos making the doorman's trousers tent from the start of an erection. She grabbed for the car door handle, yanking it open and plopping heavily on

The Sacrifice

the slippery, leather seat.

Barrex raised an inquisitive brow at his beautiful sister. His glanced at her lap where her coat had parted, revealing an alarmingly short, black leather dress and garter belts attached to black stockings where they rested on her mid-thigh.

"Well, hell! No point asking where you want to go," he snorted. "Feeling a bit like the Domme tonight?"

She gave him a petulant glare. "You know I only hunt in the underground clubs. Why waste time bumping and grinding to tasteless music all night?" She pulled the hem of her coat together. "And I'm always the Domme."

Barrex smiled in admiration. "People don't say bumping and grinding anymore. God, what would you do without me? It's twerking now. Anyway, you look amazing. Wonder who the lucky guy will be."

"I won't kill him, if that's what you're thinking."

"Of course, you won't. Your stereotypical, movie character morals are so nauseating," he rolled his eyes at his sister's absurd reverence for all life. "But you need to. I mean it, Blue, you need to. You're too weak."

He knew, even as he pleaded with her to take a life to save her own, his plea was falling on deaf ears. It had become his role throughout the

Christy Lynn

centuries to look out for his baby sister. He never begrudged it, he loved her with all his heart. But at times like this, he wanted to shake her until her teeth rattled for making his life more difficult than it had to be.

Barrex understood Brigid. He knew why she fell into these paralyzing, depressive valleys. Heck, he could just as easily do the same, if not for his role in Brigid's life, and the promise he made to their mother to take care of his little sister. Brigid's moments of sadness were the reason he nicknamed her Blue. When they first began discovering they were unique in this world and Brigid started locking herself in their home back in Ireland to keep from draining the dear lads she so desired, their mother told her that her grief was the most melancholy, lovely shade of blue.

CHAPTER 2

Brother and sister, a deadly, sensual duo, strolled into the private, BDSM club arm-in-arm. Those near the entrance turned to see who had just walked in. Brigid's need was so strong, people felt the pair before they even came into view.

They paused at the outer edge of the dance floor, watching the general chaos of it all and letting the deep bass of the music jumpstart their adrenaline. Immediately, a young man appeared in front of Barrex, dropping to his knees and bowing his head. Barrex was a well-known patron of the establishment, and a favorite among the male, submissive crowd; known for his creative torture techniques. Barrex looked down at the kneeling man then grinned at Brigid, chuckling sadistically.

She started to laugh, as well, but the smile froze on her face when Barrex seized the sub by the arm, yanked him to his feet, swatted him hard on the backside, and pointed for him to leave. "Why did you do that? He was cute."

Barrex shrugged. "You might be feeling dominant tonight, lil' sis, but I am not."

Brigid shook her head, grinning at her big brother. Barrex, being her older brother, was

Christy Lynn

actually only twelve hours older than she. By definition, they were paternal twins, not identical. Their mother gave birth to Barrex at exactly midnight of the New Year of fourteen-hundred-fifty-six. It was an easy birth. But she labored over Brigid for twelve hours longer, delivering her at precisely high-noon, New Year's Day.

Barrex Whelan was one of the most eligible, unobtainable bachelors in New York society; as well as every other society in the world he had managed to infiltrate throughout the centuries. His charm and charisma drew male - and female - alike to his side like a Chihuahua to ankles. His mother named him after the Celtic god of war, saying in a teasing manner that she knew the god personally.

His hair was dark as a moonless night and his eyes as deep brown as a wolf; which is the meaning of their last name, Whelan. Those fathomless eyes gave the false impression of softness and kindness, which in most situations, Barrex was both. However, during times of coupling, the kindness of his eyes was a deadly deception. He was ruthless in the bedroom - just like his twin sister.

Where Barrex was dark, Brigid was light. Her hair, thick and hanging past her elbows, resembled a strong batch of clover honey held to the sun, and her eyes a most unusual shade of greenish-yellow, were like those of a feline. Her

The Sacrifice

mother named her after the Celtic goddess of healing, claiming the Goddess was her favorite to read about as a little girl.

Their mother was a simple, but strong, woman. Born into a family of Gaelic warriors. She was mortal in every sense of the word, and owed her extensive knowledge of the Ancients to her own mother's devotion to her education in a time when educating women was scorned.

Melancholy and moody when not experiencing intimacy with humans on a regular basis, Brigid began living as a hermit over the years in attempt to save those she could from her irresistible, deadly appeal. But what good is being immortal if one cannot truly live life? And what is life without being able to share it with someone you love?

Barrex headed off into the dancing throng, Brigid smiling to herself as she watched him. He always hunted in the same pattern; dancing around for a few moments, bumping into people and tapping small amounts of their adrenaline to gain strength for whomever he decided to feed from in earnest.

To her relief, she had managed to make him promise in the car that he wouldn't kill some innocent submissive tonight. A thought occurred to her and her smile faded. He promised not to kill a submissive, but he just confessed he wasn't feeling dominant tonight, therefore, he wouldn't be playing with a sub. Surely, he wouldn't kill a dominant because of a play on words?

Brigid exhaled forcibly through her nostrils and decided there was nothing she could do. If he was going to drain humans until air no longer passed through their lungs, then there was no stopping him. So, she decided she better get on with the unsettling business of hunting and scanned the large, dark room for a submissive waiting for a dominant to play with.

At first glance, no one seemed available, so she went to the bar to wait. "Cranberry juice, please."

The bartender gave her an awkward smile. "There's a two-drink maximum at this club. You are allowed at least some alcohol." Most underground sex clubs served no alcohol at all, wanting to guarantee that everyone was of a clear, consenting mind when playing within the establishment walls.

Brigid nodded and smiled at the man. "I know, thank you." She reached her hand across the bar and laid it on his wrist. "Cranberry juice, please," she repeated.

The bartender's face softened at her touch and he stopped his constant moving to take time to look at her, suddenly interested. Quickly, she pulled back, silently cursing herself for being so desperate as to swipe a little energy from a staff member...good way to bring attention to oneself.

The Sacrifice

"Hi."

Brigid turned slowly on her barstool with drink in hand to see who had spoken to her. She nearly choked on the juice she was sipping through a thin, cocktail straw when she saw the man in front of her. It wasn't often she was instantly attracted to anyone; she rarely even looked at a victim's face anymore, not wanting to carry those she depleted in her memories. But this man was stunningly sexy! His presence was nearly a physical force that she felt in her gut; a feeling she couldn't decide was pleasant or disturbing.

He was noticeably tall. His frame blocked the lights from the dance floor, putting his face in shadow, but the little bit of it she could see without squinting unattractively, was handsomely defined. He had a five o'clock shadow that gave him a roguish appearance, and his black hair was perfectly messy; like a model in a Guess Jeans ad.

She straightened her shoulders, suddenly interested in playing with her food. Was it the combination of darkness and black lights, or were his eyes deep blue? She had a thing for blue-eyed men. The trait became a preference for her because she lost her virginity to a man with eyes as blue as the Caribbean Sea. She leaned forward slightly, trying to get a better look, then realized she was staring.

Christy Lynn

"Hello," she finally answered.

The man gave her a lopsided grin, no doubt wondering what she was staring at. But it was a grin so hot and endearing, she became damp just from looking at it. His wide mouth was perfectly kissable and seemed to carry a hint of humor at its corners. Brigid had been called the Devil on many occasions, and over time, had begun to believe she was; but seeing this man before her, so wickedly seductive in black jeans and black t-shirt, she knew she could no longer own the title of Mistress of the Damned - because Satan himself had somehow escaped the confines of Hell and was looking at her with eyes that suggested a thousand sinful things he wanted to do to her.

"May I buy you another drink?" Brigid laughed lightly at his joke; the jest being juice was free at the bar.

Suddenly, she felt a scalding pain shoot across her abdomen, a sure sign her succubus nature had been far too long neglected. "Are you alright?" the man asked, true concern in his eyes.

Quickly, Brigid composed herself and decided she had better get down to business. "Yes, I'm fine, thank you. I'm Brigid," she held her hand out in welcome, then hesitated in horror at her error; never give anyone your real name! She was simply known as The Mistress on the scene.

The man took her small hand in his large palm and raised it to his lips, kissing the sensitive flesh

The Sacrifice

between the first and second knuckles. It caught her off guard, men simply didn't do that in this day and age. The last time a gentleman kissed her hand was in eighteen-ninety-seven during an introduction with Brigadier General, Gregory Cole of the British Army.

His lips lingered a moment against her skin, soft and lush. His light, warm breath gently tickled the back of her hand, and she swore she could feel his exhalations all the way to her nipples. A strange feeling, like static electricity, made the hairs on her forearm stand on end.

"I'm Den," he said, in a voice much too sultry and deep. She felt the intimate muscles of her sex clench just from the sound of it.

"Den?" Brigid gave him a look. "That's a terrible fake name." Quickly, she removed her hand from his grasp.

She noticed him watching her lips as she spoke. He leaned closer to be heard over the loud music, and Brigid was caught off guard when her knees went slightly weak at the scent of his cologne. He smelled of the forest, with a hint of basil and, perhaps, Dial soap?

"It isn't fake. My name is Dennis Markham. Everyone calls me Den." He straightened back up and Brigid nearly fell forward trying to follow his smell.

Awkwardly, she regained her posture, blinking rapidly in concern. What was wrong with

Christy Lynn

her? She never acts like this toward anyone. "You really shouldn't tell people in places like this your true identity; especially your last name."

Her cheek started to gently burn where his five o'clock shadow had grazed it. Gingerly, she touched the small area with her fingertips, hoping her face wasn't red. Her thoughts were racing, trying to rationalize the strange attraction she was feeling toward this man she'd just met.

Instantly, she found an answer that was satisfactory, and she felt herself relax. It had simply been too long since her arousal was sated; good old succubus hunger, plain enough. All she needed was to ride this hunk of man hard enough to break his cock in two. Yes, that was it! This insane draw to this stranger named Dennis Markham was only a side effect of chi withdrawal.

Den shrugged his shoulders, looking around at the crowd. "Why not? No one cares what my name is. Besides, I can handle myself."

Looking at his physique, she had no doubt he could. Absently, she licked her bottom lip, imagining sitting on those broad shoulders as that five o'clock shadow chafed her inner thighs. No doubt, his large, strong hands could deliver a fantastic spanking. Immediately, her lustful thoughts came to a screeching halt...a spanking? Did she, always the Domme, just fantasize about receiving punishment from this sexy stranger?

"That man you came here with, are you

The Sacrifice

together?" Den asked, reaching for a bottle of beer the bartender left sitting on the bar for him.

"In a sense, I suppose. He's my brother."

Den tipped the bottle back and took a small sip. As he swallowed, Brigid's gaze followed the movement of his throat muscles to the neckline of his shirt; disappointed it didn't reveal more of his chest but did show a few dark hairs. She loved a small patch of hair on a man's chest.

"Brother? Good." His breath carried the faint, intoxicating smell of hops and brew.

Brigid caught sight of a small tattoo on his right wrist when he had tipped his beer for a drink. They were demons, wrapped intimately around one another; ghostly beautiful, rising from a paranormal mist. The look of them left no doubt they were prison tattoos; faded, blue ink with rough outlines from the method of 'stick and poke' so popular behind bars. She also knew that a demon signified the soul of a person whose life ended by your own doing - he had two.

Why was she always attracted to the bad boys?

Just then, a tall blonde rudely wedged her way between them, her back to Brigid. It wasn't clear to Brigid the exchange that happened between the man and the Barbie look-alike, but the woman suddenly knelt and bowed her head, waiting for Den to accept her for use.

Brigid's succubus jealousy unexpectedly reared its dangerous head, and before she could

Christy Lynn

stop, she grabbed the woman's hair and fisted a handful of it. How dare this woman! It was plainly obvious Den was speaking with her, so why try to steal his attention? The blonde didn't look up, didn't move. Brigid was struggling so hard to control her temper her teeth were grinding painfully. It suddenly occurred to Brigid this woman could be his full-time sub, or wife, for all she knew. She knew nothing at all about this guy, yet her jealousy was so easily roused over him; interesting. She shook it off and managed to leave the woman unharmed; a little disoriented maybe from a sudden loss of chi she had no idea she was donating, but unscathed, nonetheless.

When Brigid finally released her grip, shoving the blonde's head forward, the tall woman slowly rose to her feet. She turned to Brigid, hazel eyes filled with hot passion, and softly kissed her on the lips. "May I serve you, Mistress?" she quietly begged, flashing an alluring smile.

Brigid smiled patronizingly in return and shook her head. "I'm busy at the moment, as you can see, and you are interrupting. I'll find you later. Be sure you are available."

"Yes, Mistress! I'll wait for you." The woman hurried off without another word, and without so much as a glance in Den's direction. Brigid suddenly found herself face to face with a thoroughly confused man.

"What just happened?" Den asked as he

The Sacrifice

watched the blonde submissive disappear into the thick haze from a fog machine being used near the demonstration area.

Brigid innocently shrugged. "Sometimes it just takes a woman's touch, I guess," she smiled coyly.

"Oh no, little minx, you're not getting off that easily." He pointed to the floor. "Kneel."

Den's command shocked her. Her brows rose defiantly, and she batted her lashes. "Kneel? Oh, darling, I don't think so."

Brigid was suddenly uncomfortably surprised to find herself at odds. When this man commanded her to kneel, she truly felt the urge to do so. She was not a submissive and could not imagine ever submitting to a man, especially a human. But, this man...he had a powerful vibe that made her want to please him.

"If you think I'm going to kneel for you, little minx, think again." The deep gravel of his voice caused a shiver to trickle down her spine, and she could feel that familiar pull between her thighs.

No! she thought. Oh, god, no!

She realized, quite suddenly, just how badly she wanted to have sex with him. Her body was screaming to feel his weight on her as he took her, giving her the part of himself she desperately needed to survive. As hungry as she was - as aroused - there was no way she would be able to control herself, and Dennis Markham would be

Christy Lynn

dead in a matter of minutes.

She felt suddenly awkward. Why had this man, who was obviously a seasoned dominant, mistaken her for a sub? It bothered her more than it should have. Nervously, she glanced around the club, trying to withdrawal from the conversation in order to regain her focus. But it seemed Dennis Markham would have no part of her focus being anywhere but on him. Gently, he took her hand, pulling her attention back to him. He rubbed his thumb over her knuckles, staring evenly into her eyes; again, that thrum of electricity!

"Would you like to come with me?" he asked, his eyes rolling suggestively toward the dark hallway that led to the private rooms.

Her heart began pounding in her ears and she could barely breathe. *Hell yes, I want to come with you...on top of you...under you...*

"Brigid!"

Suddenly, Anne appeared out of nowhere, draping her long, willowy arms around Brigid's shoulders. Quickly, Brigid pulled her hand from Den's grasp. *What in the hell is she doing here?*

CHAPTER 3

Brigid cleared her throat and forced a fake smile. "Hello, Anne."

"So good to see you, little dove!" Anne planted an exaggerated kiss on Brigid's cheek, then turned her attention to Den, "Please, pardon my intrusion. I haven't seen my bestie in weeks."

Brigid nearly vomited in her mouth. Bestie?

"Who's your friend?" Anne peeled herself from Brigid's shoulders and moved closer to Den. Quite unexpectedly, she wrapped those spidery arms around his waist like a python, having to crane her neck to look up at him, even at her height of five feet, nine inches tall.

"No friend of mine, I don't know him," Brigid lied.

"Richard," Den extended his hand and graciously shook Anne's. Brigid smiled to herself, pleased he gave Anne a false name.

"So, your name is Dick? Wonderful," Anne laughed, seductively. "I'm Annaline Fainn, but you may call me Anne." She gave his strong, solid torso a squeeze. "Any friend of Brigid's is a friend of mine."

"A Swede, eh?" Den found himself warming up to this newcomer. She had the loveliest strawberry hair; he was always attracted to

Christy Lynn

redheads and ballsy, confident women; Annaline Fainn was definitely both.

"How did you know I'm Swedish?" Anne smacked him playfully on the chest, obviously pleased at his guess of her nationality.

Den's mouth opened to answer, but he glanced at Brigid. She must have looked displeased, regardless of the tight smile stretching her full lips. Smoothly, he untangled himself from Anne's grasp and took a single step away. He straightened his shoulders and cleared his throat. "Can I get you something from the bar, Anne?"

Anne casually dismissed Den's offer, then gave Brigid another hug. "It's been real. Come by the Tower, your cleaning staff is bored with nothing to do. Surely, you haven't forgotten you live there?" she whispered the latter, her tone resounding a warning.

The cold smile melted from Brigid's face, replaced by an icy glare, which Anne wisely chose to ignore. Suddenly, Anne stepped close to Den once more. "It was a pleasure meeting you, Dick." She stood on her tiptoes and whispered something in his ear.

Brigid watched closely, shaking her head in disgust. Sure enough, Anne was compelling the man. How dare she, when it was perfectly clear Brigid had targeted him as prey? Anne held tight to his right hand, placing her other hand on the back of his neck, no doubt letting her breath tickle

The Sacrifice

his earlobe, as her pheromones tickled his nose. Brigid knew the touch, knew how sensitive a man's palms and neck were; and knew above all else, the scent of a succubus's pheromones was impossible to ignore.

Without a backward glance, Annaline Fainn dissolved into the crowd. Brigid watched as Den's gaze followed her. She knew that look. "It was nice to meet you, Brigid. I hope to see you again soon. I really do."

She couldn't be angry at him for taking Anne's apparent offer to play in one of the private rooms in the back of the club. The man had no choice; he was compelled by a succubus. Why hadn't she intervened and stolen him back? Probably because Anne was, by all rights, the Head Succubus of the coven. Even if she could have charmed Den and broken Anne's spell, she'd have hell to pay tomorrow.

As hungry as she was, Brigid had the overwhelming urge to run out of the club. She just wanted to go home. But why should it bother her so much that this man would more than likely die by Anne's touch? She didn't know him from Adam, yet, there was something there...something she'd never felt.

"Surprise!" Barrex's familiar voice caught her attention above the roar of the club.

Brigid looked up, giving him a weak smile. "Why aren't you kneeling for some gross, sweaty

Christy Lynn

beefcake? Go play, Barry, that's what we're here for." She waved her hand, as if shooing a fly.

He tried to look offended. "Why is it you always describe the men I'm with as sweaty beefcakes, but your fucks are princes? Anyway, brought you a present."

Barrex jerked on a leash he was holding in his hand and a young man at the other end of it lowered himself quickly to his knees. "How may I serve you, Mistress?" the man had to practically yell over the noise for Brigid to hear.

Barrex gave her a brief hug. "I saw what Anne did. It wasn't right, Blue. She had to have done it to spite you, because you never show interest in anyone. And let me tell you, you were definitely interested in that guy! Who could blame you? He is gorgeous. Who is he?"

Brigid gave him a defeated look. "It doesn't matter now. Thanks for the gift."

She took the leash, not even bothering to mention the slave at the opposite end of the chain wasn't her taste at all. But at this point, it didn't matter; she needed to have sex now. And after the exchange with Dennis Markham, no other man in the club would have appealed to her, anyway.

"Up!" She commanded.

***

The private, back room was empty, with the

The Sacrifice

exception of hooks, chains, and a sad, sparse display of punishing equipment hanging on the far wall. There was a mattress in the corner, which Brigid eyed suspiciously. No way would she go near that thing. The bass of the club music vibrated through the plaster but was pleasantly muted in comparison to the bar area, giving Brigid time to breathe and process what had taken place.

After a few moments of facing the wall to compose herself, she turned to face Barrex's thoughtful gift. "Present yourself," she coldly commanded. There would be no friendly exchanges with this one. This was purely survival.

The slave immediately knelt at her feet, spreading his knees apart so his cock and balls dangled for her viewing pleasure. He clasped his hands behind his back and made sure his gaze remained on the concrete floor.

"Very good, you've been trained," she observed.

"Does that please you, Mistress?"

"No, not really. I did not give you permission to speak," Brigid snapped. She saw the man's face flinch. "However, I didn't say you couldn't speak, either. I'll forgive the error this once. Do not speak unless commanded." She sighed, feeling that tender pity she always feels for the victim she is about to seduce.

"What is your name?" she asked.

Christy Lynn

"Thor," the skinny, small man replied.

Brigid didn't mean to, but she laughed out loud. This man was anything but the image of the demigod, Thor. He couldn't weigh more than one-hundred-thirty pounds soaking wet. "Why did you choose that name?"

"I didn't. It was given to me by my first master. With all due respect, Mistress, you will understand the name once my cock is hard."

She glanced again at the display of private parts hanging halfway down the man's thigh. "It's not hard...?" she whispered, not realizing she was speaking out loud.

"No, Mistress, but it's getting there." He grinned mischievously.

With his gaze securely on the floor, Thor couldn't see the surprised look that flitted across Brigid's face. She smiled to herself, unable to keep from liking this scrawny fellow. He reminded her of that little Elf on a Shelf character; that same soft, brown hair parted on the side and large, brown eyes that looked as soft as his hair. She stood in front of him for several moments, fighting internally with her decision to drain this particular human. He seemed so fragile. Surely, she would kill him before he even stuck his cock in her.

The slave at her feet was struggling to remain perfectly still in the uncomfortable position of kneeling on concrete. It drew her attention back

The Sacrifice

to the here and now, and she suddenly gasped when she saw his erect cock. It was hanging all the way to the cold floor, the head bending slightly from lack of room. It may have been her imagination, but that thing had to be at least twelve inches long!

"Well, well," she cleared her throat. "I suppose your nickname is appropriate, after all."

Just then, Brigid decided to dismiss this adorable, submissive man in order to save him from possible harm. She was too famished to be trusted. Her body was screaming for the chi so available at her feet. A cold sweat was making her palms clammy and her clitoris was throbbing. She couldn't tear her gaze from the fat, long shaft stretching downward like a third leg from the man's torso.

Tentatively, she reached out to stroke his hair, but saw her hand shaking violently. This was incredibly stupid, Thor was obviously a favorite to some dominant who took the time to nurture and mentor him. She had meant it when she told him his training did not please her. In other words, someone would notice if he came up missing.

Before the last drop of strength she possessed vanished, Brigid walked quickly to the far wall, pretending to inspect the row of floggers and whips. "Leave," she ordered, suddenly.

"Mistress?" Thor questioned, his voice mournfully confused.

Christy Lynn

"Trust me, it's better you go now." Her throat had gone dry, making her voice raspy.

"Mistress," he started softly. "I know I'm not a big, hulk of a man, but I can handle a lot more than you think. If you're worried about blood play or being too brutal," he paused. "Or do you think I may not please you? I will! You'll be surprised at my skills in oral."

She was trembling all over, her sex wet and beyond needy. But it was better this way, little Thor would not be able to...Tap! Tap! Tap! There was a light, quick knock at the door and Brigid thought she would faint with relief.

She practically ran to answer it, sweeping past Thor, who was still kneeling; refusing, for once, to obey a direct command. "Why are you still here?" she barked, not pausing to wait for an answer.

She yanked open the door and there, in the dark hallway, was the blonde submissive she had sent away with the promise of a later liaison. Without hesitation, Brigid grabbed her by the arm and yanked her into the room. Thor may not be able to satisfy her need on his own, but if she fed from two submissives, no one would have to die!

Skipping all the pleasantries, Brigid pushed the blonde to her knees and shoved her head between her thighs. Her pretty face disappeared underneath the hem of Brigid's short, black dress. Immediately, the sub began sucking and licking. It felt so good. The expression on Brigid's face

The Sacrifice

changed to one of cold, cruel intent; the look she possesses when feeling suddenly sadistic.

The urges were building. She fisted the woman's hair and smashed her face into her wet readiness, grinding her hips and fucking her mouth. With her free hand, Brigid snapped her fingers and pointed behind her. Thor jumped to attention, scrambling to obey.

He positioned himself behind her, and she desperately tried to suppress the sigh in her throat when his cock brushed her rounded bottom. She felt the stickiness of semen when a long string of pre-cum stretched from the tip of his cock to the tender underside of her perfect ass, and the connection spurred her onward.

Brigid arched her back, pushing the blonde's face with her, making sure her mouth stayed securely sealed on her throbbing clit. She pressed her backside against Thor's pelvis. He lifted his heavy member with his right hand, gripping her hip with his left. She inhaled sharply at the searing stretch his girth created inside her; little Thor would be someone she would remember, a cock his size simply did not come along often.

Den's face flashed before her eyes. She moaned, imaging it was him filling her. She was tempted to contemplate why, after only a brief meeting of perhaps fifteen minutes, she was fantasizing about him; but this was not the time. In this moment, it was the flesh in charge, not the

Christy Lynn

mind, so she pushed him from her thoughts.

Brigid's succubus nature could plainly see that both submissives felt the raw force of her arousal, could smell it like a shark smells a drop of blood in a square mile of saltwater. All awareness seemed to escape them in a blissful rush. They became the mindless slaves a starving succubus needed; willingly giving every ounce of their precious life force through their most sacred and vulnerable areas.

Blind with lust, Brigid dropped to her knees. Thor, momentarily one with his Mistress, stayed inside her, unable to stop his determined thrusts. Each time he withdrew, he was able to fill her deeper and deeper, inch by inch. She pushed the blonde onto her back and buried her face into the sweet girl's hot depths, consuming her as if she were a meal.

Closer and closer, Brigid crept toward her climax. Her strength was returning, and she was suddenly ecstatic; in love with life and all its pleasures. Her depression and gloom lifted, pushed aside by the tender lust filling her veins. She could feel her own sensuality, intoxicating and addicting to those foolish enough to be ensnared by it. Her demonic nature emerged from its dark depths, and she could feel her morality slipping away...who cared if they died?

She felt the surge of felicity while her body hungrily absorbed the energy of her willing

The Sacrifice

donors. A gasp of ecstasy slipped out in a whisper as the feeling of being filled overwhelmed her. Harder she pushed against Thor's enormous cock, her muscles clenching, squeezing it like a Chinese finger trap. She would exorcise every drop of his semen, no matter the cost.

The blonde's essence was salty and sweet, tempting Brigid to drink her dry. She could taste the woman's chi as it filled her mouth, her nostrils. The current of it, so strong and fresh at first, was beginning to wane. She sucked harder, trying to draw more.

Please, not yet, her thoughts cried.

Thor's enthusiastic pounding was becoming softer, his body weight heavy, and he started to lean on Brigid's back. The subs were tiring; dying. Brigid's rational mind mercifully gave a final effort to stop her from finishing them off.

Using what little willpower she had left, she sat up, pulling her impaled body from the drained cock still hard and buried deep within. As tired as the blonde was, she tried to reach for Brigid, not wanting to be without the succubus's kiss. But her arms fell limp at her sides and her eyes closed.

"Here, lay down," Brigid panted, softly commanding Thor. She helped him stretch out next to the Blonde's drained body.

"Mistress, you wore me out," Thor chuckled, smiling faintly at Brigid. "God, you're so beautiful." Lazily, he turned his head toward the

Christy Lynn

blonde sub at his side. "Have you ever seen a Mistress so beautiful?"he asked.

"How do you feel?" Brigid nervously eyed the form of the woman. She was so still Brigid couldn't even see the rise and fall of her chest to gauge if she was breathing. Had she survived?

Her eyes were closed, but she smiled and formed the "ok" symbol with her thumb and index finger. Brigid laughed out loud, suddenly elated. She did it, mastered her primal nature and left no casualties!

CHAPTER 4

For years, the coven had been talking about leasing the first ten floors of the Tower for commercial use and by the number of pedestrians in the huge, marble lobby it was obvious to Brigid they had finally decided to do so. She stopped just inside the entrance, staring at the buzzing chaos as it swarmed around her.

"Miss Whelan!" Marshall Murphy's deep voice cut through the hum of the crowd. "It's so good to see you, ma'am."

Brigid beamed at the head of security, taking his hand and shaking it warmly. Alarmed, she glanced down at their joined palms. "Where are your gloves?" she whispered, giving him a stern glare. Immediately, she jerked her hand from his grasp. Nervously, she glanced around to see if anyone had overheard.

All staff hired by the coven to work at the Tower wore protective barriers, such as gloves and long-sleeved shirts. Most of them had no idea why there was a strictly enforced dress code, but those who held more trusted positions, as Marshall did, were paid handsomely for their silence; not to mention, the penalty for disclosure was death. It was doubtful any of the staff would talk anyway; they were compelled by the Head

Christy Lynn

Succubus, herself, and most of them were desperately in love with her.

Marshall balled his hand into a fist and shoved it into his pocket. "Miss Fainn requested several of us not wear our gloves until further notice."

"Oh? When did that happen?"

"A few months ago, Miss Whelan." He smiled kindly at the disturbed look on her face. "It's been six months since you were last home, ma'am, a lot has changed."

Brigid frowned, unable to remember the last time she had popped in to check on her condominium. She didn't care about the place at all, so why bother visiting? It was on her agenda for the day to send a group email to the entire coven, proposing they allow her to sell her apartment back to them at the original price she paid. Considering the boost in status of the area, the current market value was approximately worth fourteen times what it was when she bought it, so the coven shouldn't protest the sale; there was just too much equity to be gained.

"I see we have commercial tenants now," she casually remarked, waving a dismissive hand at the surge of bodies churning around them.

"Haven't you noticed the increased revenue from your resident's co-op?" Marshall asked.

Brigid shrugged, nonchalantly. She stopped looking at her accounts in the eighteen hundreds, when she funded a gold mining expedition to the new state of Oregon. It turned out to be a very wise investment. Since then, a private firm handled the rest.

Marshall offered his arm, which Brigid accepted politely. She liked Marshall, always had. Stealthily, she glanced up at him, feeling a cold realization wash over her upon taking note of his appearance. Anne, or someone from the coven, had obviously been feeding from the staff.

"Marshall, are you feeling alright?" she asked, trying hard to keep the tone of suspicion from her voice.

Six months ago, he had rich, brown hair and clear, tight skin. A healthy, full beard had covered his jaw and there was a sparkle in his eyes that showcased his love of life. This person at her side was a shadow of that man. His hair was dull, streaked with a lifeless gray. The beard was gone, shaved clean, revealing a pale complexion. Laugh lines and crow's feet had managed to etch themselves on the smooth planes of his face, and his eyes held the tell-tale, dull glaze of a succubus's snack.

"I'm fine. Just a little tired these days," he chuckled and patted her hand where it rested in the crook of his elbow. "Don't trouble yourself, ma'am, been to the doctor Mistress Anne was kind enough to refer me to, and he says I'm healthy as an ox. We all get old."

"Anne referred him, eh? I bet that's exactly

Christy Lynn

what the doctor said. Well, maybe now that the building is full of...tenants...Anne will let you put your gloves back on," Brigid quipped.

Always the devotee, Marshall kept the broad smile on his face as he made some comment about not minding if she didn't. Brigid rolled her eyes; no doubt the man wouldn't mind. Being drained of one's chi by a succubus was an incredibly erotic experience that tended to leave the victim trapped in a false sense of deep devotion and love. Marshall was obviously in the throes of both with Anne; had been since the day she hired him.

The two of them walked past a row of six elevators, which were filling up quickly, to a private one around the corner from the main lobby. They stepped inside, chatting idly. When the door slid silently closed, Marshall inserted his key for the penthouse.

"Oh, I'm sorry, Marshall, but I'm not here to see Anne. I'm just checking on my staff."

Marshall nodded patiently. "Miss Fainn has requested to see you, Miss Whelan."

Brigid clamped her jaw shut, her teeth pressing into the well-worn pattern engraved over time. The last person she wanted to see right now was Annaline Fainn, especially after the bitch stole Dennis Markham from under her nose the night before. The fact that he was still in her thoughts at all, was unnerving enough as it was. She'd spent the better part of the morning beating

The Sacrifice

herself up for thinking of him, for wondering what it was about that gorgeous man that had her so confounded. And what was that feeling of electricity whenever he touched her?

"Marshall, I'm sure I don't need to tell you twice. I have no desire to see Anne. I'm going to my condo." She tried to sound as stern as possible but knew her tone was as hollow as its underlying threat. She would never do anything to harm him, and he knew it.

Marshall's ever-present smile faded, and his gaze shifted to the display above the elevator door as it counted the floors they were passing. Brigid and Barrex had apartments on the floor directly below the penthouse, showing their status in the coven. They passed them, the elevator slowing as it prepared to stop.

"Hey, I'm talking to you," Brigid snapped.

"Miss Whelan, I'm just doing my job."

"Of course, you are," she huffed.

The door opened, and with a heavy sigh of dread, Brigid stepped into Anne's enormous penthouse. The midday sun was reflecting off the marble flooring, momentarily blinding her. Manhattan was breathtaking from this height and she couldn't help but pause to admire the urban view. The ding of the elevator doors closing surprised her, and she whirled around in time to see that Marshall did not exit with her.

"Brigid, how are you?" Anne breezed into the

foyer, an ivory-colored, silk robe flowing around her thin frame.

Brigid gave her an impatient look. "Well, you tell me, Anne. I came here to check on my place and was abducted by your minion."

"Nonsense," Anne giggled. "You're always so dramatic."

Brigid felt the heat rise in her cheeks. She was over six centuries old, well matured beyond getting her ire up over flippant remarks, but Anne had that effect on her. There was a time when she loved Anne more than life itself, until she told her of her part in the death of her mother. Even then, she tried to forgive her, tried to continue loving her as if she were family. But Anne's lack of remorse over the years, her unapologetic manner, filled Brigid's heart with lead.

She reluctantly followed the willowy redhead into the sitting room and took a seat in one of the smaller, stuffed chairs nearest a large wall of windows. Just then Anne's butler appeared from the kitchen. He was a beautiful, Cantonese man with long, strikingly black hair and eyes to match. He was completely naked, with the exception of an apron tied around his waist.

Brigid's left brow rose in amusement. "I apologize, I must have come at a bad time." She prepared to get up and leave, but Anne motioned hastily for her to remain seated.

"Don't be ridiculous. Anytime you want to

The Sacrifice

visit, is always a good time." Anne turned her attention to the lovely butler. "I told you to stay in the kitchen."

The olive-skinned man hurried to where Anne was lounging on a sofa and quickly knelt at her feet. "I'm sorry, Mistress. Please, forgive me? I just missed you so..."

Anne's right hand shot up, silencing the mournful begging. "Do not forget your place, Hak Gwai. You are only a servant."

Anne had given the purchased slave the name Hak Gwai when she bought him. It means black ghost, which at the time, Anne was unaware was an offensive slang name in the Cantonese culture. She thought the name was clever, considering his jet-black hair and eyes. Hak Gwai adored his mistress so much he endured the insulting name without a word.

"Only a servant?" Hak Gwai couldn't hide the pain of those words, it flashed across his face like a spasm. His mouth formed the words as his eyes dropped from Anne's hard gaze to the floor.

Anne sighed, the sound dripping with frustration. She looked to Brigid as if she needed sisterly advice. "What do you do with the help when they think they are more to you than they are?"

"I don't know," Brigid quipped. "I don't have that problem in my household."

Anne's cheery facade was crumbling fast and

Christy Lynn

Brigid's rude demeanor was pressing the wrong buttons. Without another word, Anne stood and grasped a handful of the man's shiny, gorgeous hair. He winced, grabbing for Anne's wrist in attempt to stop the painful pulling. Anne ignored him and dragged him to the glass wall.

"Stand up, Hak," she hissed through clenched teeth.

Brigid moved to the edge of her seat, her senses suddenly alert. She clasped her hands nervously in her lap. "Look, I don't have time for this. You summoned me here for a reason, so get to it, or I'm leaving."

Anne dismissed her with a wave of her slender hand. "Brigid, we are immortal, we have all the time in the world. Surely, you can afford a few moments for your Head Mistress?"

The snappy response of you are not my Mistress, was hanging on the tip of Brigid's tongue. She trapped it between her teeth, smart enough to know when to be quiet. Annaline Fainn was hundreds of years older - and centuries stronger.

"Now, my little treasure," Anne's calculating gaze returned to the chiseled man, who was now standing naked against the glass wall, back turned toward the room, revealing a perfectly rounded backside. "I think you need a reminder of your place in this house."

"But you said you loved me," Hak Gwai began

The Sacrifice

to sob, his thin body trembling.

"So?" Anne snapped.

Brigid's stomach turned sour from Anne's callousness. She couldn't help but wonder if Anne had treated Den in such a cruel fashion. Did he die happy, as a victim should in the hands of a succubus? She didn't think to check any news for a report on a possible homicide; but this was New York City, it was highly unlikely a corpse found in a dumpster behind an underground, BDSM club would make the news. Besides, Anne would've had his body professionally taken care of, leaving no evidence.

The sharp sound of leather meeting flesh startled Brigid from her morose thoughts of Dennis Markham's demise. She looked up in time to see Anne roughly squeezing Hak Gwai's ass. A telltale, red mark from a strap that stretched across both cheeks was darkening quickly, accompanied by a rising welt.

The butler's palms pressed flat against the cool glass, his slender fingers stretching in response to the bite of the strap, then curling into fists. Anne grinned wickedly at Brigid then took another swing with the thick belt. Brigid bit into her lower lip, pressing her thighs tightly together against her stirring desire. She could see Hak Gwai's erection in the reflection of the window, and it called to her.

"Damn it," she muttered. The last thing she

needed was to find herself in the grip of arousal while in Anne's presence.

Again, the strap came down with a sharp crack! The butler's knees bent as he writhed in painful ecstasy. "Do I love you, Hak?" Anne asked, her tone teasing and ruthless.

The man choked on his tears, his Cantonese accent heart wrenchingly mournful from the discipline. "No, Mistress, you do not love me. I am only a servant," he wept.

"What?" Anne's voice rose in mock anger. "How dare you say such a thing? I give you everything you want, ungrateful bastard! I let you sleep on the floor by my bed. I've even said I love you. What a disappointment!"

Brigid winced as she saw how far Anne drew back her arm for the final swing of the belt. It landed solidly across the man's bottom, eliciting a loud cry so agonizing it seemed to come from the depths of the poor servant's soul. Unable to stand another minute of the flogging, Hak Gwai slid to the cold, marble floor; a sobbing heap.

With her anger finally sated, Anne let the belt drop to the floor and shook her arms as if she'd just completed an hour long session of lifting free weights. Brigid watched, nearly panting with desire. She wanted nothing more than to feel the heat from that freshly spanked ass; to hold the small, beautifully exotic man in her arms while sucking the agony from his red lips. But this was

The Sacrifice

not her place and Anne would have the pleasure of savoring the delicious lust of her victim.

"Go, wait in my bedroom," Anne snapped. She stared at her butler, pointing toward a set of ornate, French doors on the opposite side of the large room. "Now!"

Brigid exhaled quietly, relieved this was over. She knew Anne was just showing off, exerting her authority in front of her. If the butler was gone, this uncomfortable visit could move forward.

Hak Gwai looked up at Anne, fat tears teetering on his lower lashes. "Mistress, please," he whispered. "Let me remain near you. I can't stand when you are angry with me."

Anne's jaw set itself firmly and in a way that transformed her features into fearsome, sharp angles. Brigid saw the man's shoulders shaking from sobs that had erupted anew. Nervously, she fished her cell phone out of her pocket and pretended to read a text so Anne would have privacy to deal with this situation. She hoped if Anne saw she wasn't paying attention, she would treat Hak Gwai more gently.

A shrill cry startled her, and she dropped her phone onto the thick area rug. Thankfully, the carpeting was plush enough to save the glass screen from shattering. Brigid didn't even bother to pick it up and check, though. Her eyes were riveted on the scene before her.

"Anne, stop!" She hurried to where Anne was

Christy Lynn

knelt on the floor with Hak Gwai in her arms. She didn't see what he had done to push Anne over the edge and cause her to lose control, but whatever it was, there was no stopping her now.

Brigid didn't dare touch Anne, didn't try to grab her shoulders to drag her off the young man. If she had, it would've made things worse for him. She would've ended up drawing on his energy, as well, using Anne as a conduit, and he would perish twice as quickly. She fell to her knees next to them, attempting to get Anne's attention, anything that might distract her and bring her to her senses.

Anne's fingers were tangled in that silky, black hair; gripping it so tightly, her knuckles were white. Her mouth was pressed so hard against Hak Gwai's, it had split his lip. Brigid gasped when she saw a thin trickle of blood run down his cheek. Was Anne's anger so roused as to draw blood?

"C'mon, Annaline, that's enough! You're killing him," Brigid was to the point of begging. "It's Hak, stop!"

It was useless to plead; it was too late. All she could do was wait for Anne to end it. She was mercilessly torn; she felt weak, her body tingling with need, but at the same time, she was appalled by her old friend's cruelty. Too much time had passed without her knowing Anne, as she once did...what had happened to her?

The Sacrifice

Anne had never been particularly barbarous, that title had always been reserved for Brigid, who was often referred to as the woman without a soul. She had been one of those unfortunates who was not able to recover after her first love broke her heart, therefore making all others merely a necessity to couple with, and nothing more.

Brigid knew exactly what Anne was feeling as she absorbed every last drop of the butler's life's energy. She noticed the gooseflesh dappling Anne's forearms and knew she was experiencing that addicting elation of power. She imagined it was similar to a heroin high, from what she had heard from those who personally experienced it. She shivered, craving that rush for herself.

Slowly, Hak Gwai's depleted body slipped from Anne's lap to the floor; his limp arms were bent at chillingly grotesque angles. Brigid always hated the way bodies looked once they lost muscle tone and she shuddered at the sight of his twisted neck; the side of his face pressed against that cold marble.

She wanted to scream at Anne, ask her how she could do such a thing! But the wild look of lost reason was still prevalent in the Head Mistress's eyes. Quietly, she climbed to her feet and went to the wall of windows to stare out at Manhattan as it glistened in the midday sun. Lightly, she rubbed her neck just where it sloped to her collar bone. This was something she did when deeply

Christy Lynn

distressed; always a window, always feeling the need to escape.

CHAPTER 5

"Ok! So, where were we before we were so rudely interrupted?" Anne had composed herself and taken her seat once again.

Even Anne knew her behavior was unacceptable; she'd gone too far, but wasn't about to admit it. She cleared her throat and plucked a Hershey Kiss from a small bowl on the table next to her. "You think I would've learned from your brother," she murmured, nonchalantly.

Brigid glanced at her. "Barry? What does he have to do with any of this?" she asked, disdainfully. Her gaze swept the room, pausing on Hak Gwai's still form. A pang of sadness shot through her chest; he had been Anne's butler for two years and everyone adored him. He was such a sweet, kind man.

Anne chuckled lightly. "Surely, you haven't forgotten the fiasco with that Creole stable boy he was stupid enough to fall in love with? When was that?" Her voice drifted, getting quieter as she appeared to be thinking. "Seventeen-forty-two, wasn't it?"

"Forty-three," Brigid corrected. And yes, she did remember.

She remembered the cold, hard fear of

possibly losing Barrex forever. After the groom died, he tried to kill himself – twice. Brigid was on suicide watch for months. She experienced the first real terror in her entire life; an eternity alone without her immortal twin at her side. He was her strength, her family; what would she have done without him?

After three-hundred years of depending on him, that was the moment she realized the agony she dealt her brother every time she declared she was going to starve to death from chi withdrawal and allow herself to slip into that coma so terrorizing to all succubi. If only it would've been that easy, to simply cease to exist. Twins have a special bond and when you add eternity to the mix, it becomes as strong as titanium.

"You can't compare what you felt for Hak Gwai to what Barry felt for Raimond."

"Well, that's an unfair thing to say. You have no idea what I felt for Hak," Anne protested, her mouth falling slack in a pout.

Brigid's left brow rose in disagreement. "Fair enough, perhaps I don't know how you felt, but I do know when you love someone as deeply as Barry loved Raimond, you don't kill him for not leaving the room when commanded to do so."

"Yes, well, a cautionary tale of forbidden love, if ever there was one." Anne popped another chocolate in her mouth. "And I didn't kill Hak for not leaving the room. Do you honestly believe I

The Sacrifice

would do that? I put a lot of work into him. Christ, Brigid, the man has been a whining mess for months. You have no idea what I've been dealing with. He's been so clingy and needy. I couldn't take it anymore. I'm grateful to have you witness his behavior."

After all these years, Brigid's loyalty to her brother's deceased true love was still as fresh as it had always been, and she couldn't let the topic rest. "I still don't see the connection between you killing your butler in a fit of anger and Barrex finding the love of his life hanging from a tree in a swamp because his master killed him in a fit of rage."

"Point being, humans and immortals are not meant to mix," Anne shrugged dismissively. "Do you ever miss New Orleans?"

The question caught Brigid off guard. "Well, yes, actually, quite often. I think I miss the entire seventeenth century."

Anne snickered. "Yes, good times. I still own that gorgeous, Queen Anne mansion in the Garden District. Love that house, but it truly was a shame when the First Great Fire took our townhome. Now that place was splendid." She glanced at the dead butler. "Want to move back? I wouldn't mind a break from this city, and I miss when it was just the three of us. The coven is nice and all, but so stressful, always having to clean up the messes of others."

Christy Lynn

Brigid frowned. She didn't like the thought that she and Anne were anything alike, but it was an uncomfortable coincidence that she was just thinking the exact same thing; needing time away from New York. Images of the French Quarter in all its eighteenth-century splendor flashed through her mind. The grand carriages, which have now been reduced to expensive tourist diversions, jammed the narrow, dirt streets from Bourbon to St. Charles. Gentlemen and ladies - true ladies - in the latest Parisian fashions strolled along the avenues of the Garden District with their maids in tow.

A happy drunk could be found staggering out of any bar at any hour, and often accompanied by a prostitute hanging on his arm with her bosoms jostling over the confines of her corset. In the cool of the morning, the smell of beignets being made at Cafe Du Monde mixed with the salty, pungent, harbor breeze before the tide changed. Even the sour stink, like rotten dairy, that was ever-present in the thick, humid air played in her nose...she could remember it that well.

Yes, she admitted to herself, I miss it terribly.

"Tell me, Brigid, was it you that killed that stable boy's master? I know everyone blamed Barrex, but the Comte's murder was too beautifully vengeful for a grieving lover to have divined."

"What do you mean?" she squinted, shooting

The Sacrifice

Anne with a calculated glare. She folded her arms, leaning defensively against that huge, glass wall. Hak Gwai's handprint was still lingering on the smooth surface, just inches from Brigid's face and it made her want to cry.

"Oh, c'mon, you can tell me. I'm sure you're safe from the hangman's noose after two-hundred-something years. I will bare my soul and admit I have always admired the delicate, artistic brutality of the scene the lawmen found. You would be my idol if you were to say it was you."

Anne tossed Brigid a Kiss from the bowl. Brigid took her time unwrapping the silver foil, allowing the chocolate to melt slowly on her tongue, giving an excuse to delay her answer. Suddenly, the images of that night were before her, so clear it was as if she were back in that swamp searching for her brother, listening to the sucking and squishing of the bayou mud that pulled at her feet with every step. She had just purchased the loveliest pair of satin, slip-on mules and had worn them that night; the occasion being a ball at the estate of Comte Lubin Couturier, in the Bayou Saint John region.

"The Comte held Raimond's indenture, but the fucking bastard shouldn't have been allowed to own a pig," Brigid hadn't realized she was even speaking aloud.

Anne leaned forward in keen interest, a conspiritual grin slowly spreading across her face.

Christy Lynn

"You and I would never have consorted with such a character, if Barrex hadn't insisted. We knew him for what he was the moment we first laid eyes on him. Damn, we had gotten so good at sizing up a man. Still no one better than us, is there?"

Of course, Barrex had asked Anne and Brigid to befriend the Comte's wife, Madame la Comtesse, so they would receive invitations to parties and balls held at the estate; any opportunity to see Raimond must not be missed. "He wasn't a stable boy, by the way, he was the Head Groom." She didn't know why she felt she had to defend Raimond's memory, except that she had adored him. There were few people in history good enough to capture her lovely brother's heart, but those that did often managed to capture hers, as well.

"Same difference."

"No, it isn't. The difference of position speaks volumes of the man. Did you know he was caring for two orphaned girls he found living in an alley in the Quarter? Best we could discover was their mother had been a whore who apparently never came home one night. Raimond was a good man and I'll ask you to respect his memory."

"Yes, yes, and therefore his master deserved his fate," Anne impatiently prompted Brigid to continue her confession.

Reluctantly, she did.

Barrex had left the ball an hour after it began,

The Sacrifice

heading out to the stables to find Raimond. He told Brigid he would return to the party by midnight so they could travel back to the city, since they knew it was a bad idea to stay the night, as was customary. Anne was accompanying them, she was always with them back then before she formed the coven, and to allow her to stay overnight in a room of sleeping women would've been like letting a swarm of mosquitoes loose inside a tent; the occupants would've been drained dry by sunrise.

An hour past midnight, Brigid was thoroughly worried. She went in search of the two men, only to find the barns were empty of people. She was coming out of the far end of one of the stables when she saw the Comte and two of his plantation slaves emerging from the tree line of the deep swamp that held the property's edge to the south.

Even from her position across the paddock, she could see the jerky stagger of the Comte's gait; the effect of too much wine. He was talking loudly and slapping the slaves on the back, but the two men accompanying him shared none of his joviality. Their discomfort was unmistakable to her by their rigid spines and serious faces. What had the Comte made them do to evoke such a grim manner?

Curious, she slipped along the edge of the bog and followed the narrow path, heading in the direction from which the men had just come.

Christy Lynn

Even though she had no lantern, the waxing half-moon was bright enough to guide her, still she didn't like being in the bayou in the dead of night with nocturnal reptiles on the prowl; snake venom may not be able to kill her, but it certainly could hurt like hell!

Brigid had been hurrying along, her airy, burgundy gown snagging on everything it encountered. She had glanced downward for only a moment to, yet again, yank her skirts free of a bramble, when suddenly something hard smacked her in the face, stunning her momentarily.

She stumbled backward, reaching for her injured her nose and expecting the blood to pour, which mercifully, it did not. It was going to be hard enough to explain to Anne and Madame la Comtesse where she had slinked off too in the middle of the soiree; she didn't need fresh blood splattered across her bodice to add to the intrigue and gossip.

"I thought I was going to choke on my own scream when I saw those two feet dangling in front of me," she recalled. "But it was seeing Barry propped against the base of the tree that Raimond was hanging from that frightened me most. I'd never seen his face look like that...and he was holding a knife under his own chin. He'd made sure the tip of the blade had pierced his throat in several places...so much blood."

The Sacrifice

"I've always admired how close the two of you are. Your mother made sure of it when you were growing up." Ignoring Anne was hard enough, but whenever she brought up her mother, it was impossible.

"Yes, well, imagine how much closer we would've been had our mother lived longer than our sixteen years." Brigid tried to dismiss Anne's interruption, tried to push the harbored hatred for Anne's part in her mother's death from her mind before it caused serious repercussions. For the moment, the conversation was simply for Anne's amusement, to lure her into revealing the purpose of her summons. Anything beyond that would delay this unwanted visit longer than necessary, so she inhaled deeply to regain her composure and continued for the entertainment of her hostess.

"No one knows what I went through after Raimond was murdered. Not even you," she added. A secret feeling of satisfaction curled the corners of her mouth when she saw Anne flinch from a flash of pain. She had no idea why, but Anne had never stopped trying to be an important part of her life, no matter how many years passed.

"The one question I never thought to ask is why. Why did the Comte hang Raimond?" Anne's voice was soft and she was staring at Hak's body with a strange expression in her eyes. "There's always something that pushes a person over the

Christy Lynn

edge, that one moment when all reason is lost. I never paused to wonder what it was that pushed the Comte to such a measure. I suppose I'd always assumed he did not like his property being tampered with."

Brigid nodded pensively, her gaze unfocused as she recalled the sort of man the Comte was. "You didn't know? Comte Lubin was in love with Barry. How could you not have known? He visited our home several times a month and Barry was continuously in his presence in brothels and taverns."

She tried to think of the moments surrounding the homicides, surely, she or Barrex had told Anne of Comte Lubin's infatuation with Barrex. The Comte was in constant company with Barrex, which is what led to Barrex becoming so intimately acquainted with Raimond, being the Comte's Head Groom and Factor.

The Comte had become dangerously suspicious of Barrex and Raimond, and he had a temper and jealousy befitting of a man of his stature. His own wife was terrified to give attention to any one particular individual for fear of rousing his twisted inklings. Upon discovering them the night of the ball coupled together in the seclusion of the swamp, the Comte's jealous rage found confirmation.

"I had no idea," Anne blinked. By the confounded look on her face, Brigid knew she was

The Sacrifice

telling the truth. "It makes perfect sense now. I had assumed the man was just homophobic. Turns out he was the exact opposite. Interesting."

Brigid remained silent for a few moments, recalling the horrific events that had changed her life. She found it unsettling that the actions of one man could affect her entire world for so many years. "Yes, I killed Comte Lubin Couturier. Happy?" she suddenly blurted the anticipated confession.

"Delighted!" Anne's perfect face split into a sincerely pleased smile. "Proud, more like it. Finally, after all these years, the murder is solved. You, little dove, were brilliant."

Brigid was lost again in the Bayou, completely oblivious to Anne's approval. "I wore long sleeves, as hot as it was, and silk opera gloves. I refused to allow myself to touch him. I wanted no part of that vile snake. Not an ounce of his chi passed through my skin." The far-off stare in Brigid's eyes quieted Anne momentarily. "You say it was a masterpiece, but all I was trying to do was erase the fear that man put in my soul," Brigid reminisced.

"Fear? There was nothing to suggest you bore any fear at all," Anne chuckled. "I mean, it did take the lawmen several hours to find all the pieces of his body."

Brigid took one last look at her reflection in the glass, frowning back at herself. Of the many things she had done over the centuries, the

Christy Lynn

murder of Comte Lubin Couturier was the one thing she could never bring herself to feel remorseful over.

She stepped over Hak Gwai's body on her way to a chair. "You cared for him," she remarked coolly, nodding at the corpse. "You could have used him for the sacrifice to Lilith if you had grown tired of him. He would've pleased the Goddess; such an extraordinarily beautiful man."

"Yes, he was...the best my money could buy on the Asian Black Market. But I'll get another one. The thought to offer him had crossed my mind, but thanks to you, I found the absolute perfect lamb for the altar." She smiled at Brigid, batting her eyelashes, attempting to muster a look of gratitude.

"Thanks to me?" Brigid asked tentatively. She did not want to know where this was going.

"Why, yes! That gorgeous man you introduced me to last night. What a body! Chest like a Roman soldier," Anne sighed dramatically, fanning herself as if she had suddenly become victim to a menopausal hot flash.

"You mean, Dennis?" She didn't know why, but Brigid felt her pulse quicken; the pounding in her throat an uncomfortable distraction. "He's alive?"

"Dennis? I thought his name was Richard. Anyway, what kind of woman do you think I am? You know me better than that, I don't kill every

The Sacrifice

man I'm with."Anne feigned offense. "When I got Richard - whoever the hell he is - into that back room and felt his kiss," she paused theatrically. "That man is a powerhouse of chi!"

"Really?" Brigid murmured. She was trying not to stare at Anne, trying not to look as though she was hanging on every word she was saying, but she couldn't help it. "I wouldn't think Lilith would be pleased with your sloppy seconds," she snipped.

"I know the rules, Blue," Anne answered, sarcastically calling Brigid by the nickname only her brother had permission to use. "I'm quite aware the Goddess must have a life force untainted by another succubus. I didn't have sex with him. Told him I wanted to arrange to see him again, so the first time we fucked would be mind-blowing, instead of some sleazy hookup in the back room of a club. Can you believe he was actually more than willing to wait? How refreshing to find a gentleman in a place like that."

The image of Den kissing her hand flashed through her mind; yes, a gentleman, she smiled.

Something resembling relief and anxiety simultaneously washed over Brigid. She tried to return Anne's smile, but the corners of her lips quivered. "Classy, Anne."

"Oh, my gosh! Brigid, you liked him?" Anne's remark sounded more like an accusation than a question. She tried to sound shocked, as if she

Christy Lynn

didn't know Den had been in the process of inviting Brigid for a few hours of adult fun when she had intervened.

"Like I said last night, I don't know him," Brigid flatly stated.

"I'm so sorry. I had no idea. I never would have..."

"Oh, really? You wouldn't have?" Brigid quickly stood in preparation to leave before she said something she would seriously regret. "Yes, well, there's nothing to be sorry for. I'm glad the Goddess will be pleased. Maybe she'll let you live another century...maybe."

She noticed Anne wasn't trying to delay her departure further, evidence she had told Brigid the reason for detaining her. So, all of this was to let her know Anne was planning to sacrifice Dennis Markham during the Centennial Celebration.

Anne followed Brigid to the elevator, making some remark about having Marshall take care of Hak Gwai's corpse. Her callousness made Brigid's stomach weak. Anne gave her a lazy smile. "Oh, one more thing. I didn't think you would mind, since you're never here. But, I put Dick in your condo. I didn't want to chance losing him, so I told him he could hang around here for a night or two. He thinks he's waiting to attend some exclusive, A-list party I'm throwing. I suppose, in truth, he is! I probably exaggerated the guest list a tad. He

The Sacrifice

thinks Cher is going to perform." She looked proud of her cleverness in the art of deceit.

"You did what?"

Christy Lynn

CHAPTER 6

The elevator couldn't descend the one floor to Brigid's condo fast enough, so she took the stairs – two at a time. Anne's audacity had hit an all-time low with this fiasco, and Brigid was fuming! How dare she imprison a stranger in her home without even consulting her about it? She let that be the excuse why she was so frantic to get in her apartment door, but, if truth be told, she was simply dying to see Dennis Markham once again. She had to know if what she felt the night before was her imagination, or real.

Her key slipped effortlessly into the lock, her lips forming a sardonic smile. What good was a lock when the place could be entered anytime the Head Mistress desired? As soon as she stepped inside, Den's presence smacked her like a brick wall. That cologne! Her whole place smelled faintly of him; of spices, woodlands, and clean soap.

Nothing had ever smelled more appealing. It tossed her right back to the sixteen-hundreds, when the continent was still new and wild - and so were the men. Why is it the more mankind seeks freedom, the more restrained they become?

She leaned back against the door, closing her eyes and just inhaling the heady aroma. His

The Sacrifice

leather jacket was hanging on a hook by the door right next to her and the combination of leather and manliness was intoxicating. She felt the slick paste of arousal wetting her undergarments and squeezed her thighs tightly together for stimulation. No, she couldn't do this now. She couldn't allow ardency to take over and begin the domino effect that would awaken the demons inside her. There simply wasn't time.

She swallowed hard, her throat suddenly dry. She went to the kitchen to pour a glass of water and buy some time to control her lust before finding him. She tried to remember a time when just the scent of a man excited her this much, but none came to mind.

"Oh!" she gasped, startled. She rounded the corner from the foyer into the kitchen and found herself face to face with a half-naked Dennis Markham. He was leaning against the counter with a loose pair of pajama pants hanging on his hips, and nothing else on.

His eyes grew wide. "You're the woman from the club last night. Brigid?"

She composed herself, forcing a smile. Awkwardly, she entered the space, stuffing her hands in her pockets to keep from nervously wringing them. "Yeah, you're Daniel, right?" She purposely said the wrong name in order to sound as if meeting him could barely jog her memory.

"Dennis," he corrected. "Remember, you told

Christy Lynn

me I'm not supposed to give my real name?" he answered, completely falling for it. "I don't mean to be rude, but what are you doing here? How did you get a key to my condo?"

Brigid opened her mouth to protest it being his condo, but then noticed the humor lingering on the corners of his mouth. She smiled, recalling his sense of humor. He'd offered to buy her a free drink the night before. "Actually, I should be the one asking you what you're doing here. This place is mine." She stood on her tiptoes and reached for a glass on the second shelf of one of the glass cabinets. She stretched, her fingers wiggling in hopes of making contact with an object.

Dennis quickly plucked one for her and held it in front of her face, smiling sweetly. "Oh the life of the vertically challenged," he teased.

"Thanks," she murmured. "And why are you here?"

"What? Oh, god, I'm sorry," he stammered, looking truly uncomfortable for the first time since she met him. "Anne never said anything about it belonging to someone else. I assumed it was hers. Well, you know what they say about assuming." He waved his hand to encompass the vastness of the apartment. "Beautiful place you have here."

"Thank you." Brigid took her glass of water into the living room.

She found her favorite spot near the wall of

The Sacrifice

windows and settled in, reaching for a fur throw, which had been waiting on the floor next to the loveseat, right where she preferred it. She draped it over her legs, as if she was getting comfortable for a couple hours of reading a good romance novel. Nothing could be further from her plans. She had no intention of staying in the Tower a second longer than necessary; but she would stay as long as it took to get to the bottom of this feeling she was having for Dennis Markham.

Den followed her into the large living space. He took a seat near her, still looking terribly uncomfortable. "You weren't here last night when I settled in," he began, as if explaining how he came to be in her home, but his tone eluding to fishing for information.

"No, I wasn't," she replied. Casually, she sipped the ice water and began flipping through a magazine.

"But you said this is your place," he pressed.

Brigid paused her fake interest in Vogue long enough to glance at him. "What is it you want to know, Den?"

"Is this really your home? I noticed a few pair of panties in the dresser drawer and basic toiletries in the bathroom, but no toothbrushes or anything else to suggest this place is actually lived in."

"I never said I live here, I said it's mine. I own it. Used to live here, but now I stay in my

Christy Lynn

apartment on Fifth. Wait, we're out of toothbrushes?" She had no idea why she was telling him all this, it was none of his business. The look of sudden awe on his face was so comical, she had to laugh. "What's that look for?" she giggled.

"Well," he rubbed his scruffy jaw. "You must do well for yourself. A condo on fifty-seventh, an apartment on Fifth. It's admirable."

"I do alright."

"Anyone who says they do alright is usually doing much better than that," he smiled. She noticed a single dimple in the right side of his cheek but thought it odd he didn't have one on the left side. It gave his smile an endearing uniqueness.

Brigid was covertly watching him, her eyes slipping to the bulge in his cotton pajama bottoms. It was obvious he wasn't erect, but damn, it had to be an impressive size to fill pants as baggy as those. She corrected the direction of her gaze before he caught her staring at his crotch, and for the first time, noticed a small frosting of silver highlighting the black strands of his hair. She liked men a little older; they were more of a challenge.

"Miss Whelan, welcome back, ma'am. I apologize I didn't greet you at the door. Mr. Murphy did not alert me you were home." A member of her staff had just entered the room and discovered her presence. She was checking her cell phone for any texts she might have missed from the Head of Security.

"Its fine, Layla. Mr. Murphy is busy in Miss Fainn's penthouse, I imagine." Brigid smiled warmly at the middle-aged woman but felt a sudden chill upon picturing what was happening on the floor above.

"Rest assured, I have been taking care of your guest to the best of my ability, ma'am. Are there any special requests I should be aware of?" the housekeeper stood in the archway between the living room and the hallway leading to the bedrooms. Her posture was perfect, owed to her formal training in England. Even though she was generally in the condo completely alone, she was dressed in a crisp, black uniform.

Brigid shook her head. "I'm sure he's pleased with our hospitality," she looked at Den with a questioning expression.

"Yes, thank you." He stood suddenly and stretched his back. Brigid hungrily stared at the muscles of his torso as they flexed. She loved his body type; not too buff or muscularly defined, but not too soft, either.

"If you ladies will excuse me, I'll get dressed and get out of Miss Whelan's hair." He gave Brigid a cute wink and a boyish grin.

"Don't bother trying to leave," Brigid murmured, letting the blanket on her lap fall back to its place on the floor. This was going to be a difficult conversation to have.

He paused, staring evenly at her. The tone of her voice must've given a clue that something serious was going on that he was unaware of. "Why not?" His deep tone held a note of caution.

The housekeeper, Layla, quickly disappeared from the room. She knew when she should, or should not, be present. Brigid took Den's hand to lead him to the loveseat so they could sit together. When they touched, goose bumps covered her forearms. She paused a moment, just holding onto him with her eyes closed, enjoying the sensation.

She inhaled deeply to center herself, then let her lids rise just enough to look at him. His concerned expression had relaxed, and she found him looking at her with what seemed to be a hint of curiosity...his eyes, they were deep blue! She couldn't tell for sure last night in the poor lighting of the club. Blue eyes were her favorite. How had she not noticed until now?

"What was that?" he asked.

"What was what?"

"You didn't feel that just now?" he asked, letting her hand drop as they took their seats.

She nodded but didn't say anything. Hell, yes, she felt it – and now she knew he did, too. It was like a small jolt of electricity; not in a bad way, like putting a battery to your lip, but in a gentle,

The Sacrifice

soothing way that made her feel instantly better. So, there really was something between them, it hadn't been her imagination altered by sexual depravity.

They sat together while she tried to explain to Den what he had gotten himself into. It was late afternoon and the sunlight was at the perfect angle to land on her long hair, making it look so touchable and soft. Thin, flighty, strands glowed temptingly, begging to be stroked. The color could best be described as a batch of strong, clover honey glistening in the sunlight. It accented her greenish-yellow eyes and made her appear warm and inviting. The warmth of it on her back was making her sleepy.

Den started apologizing right away for leaving her last night to go with Anne, saying he had no idea why he did it. She dismissed his apology, explaining that he really had no choice. She told him his beer had been spiked with drugs and he was abducted by an eccentric cult. It was obvious by the expression on his face he was having a hard time believing her as she told him as much as he needed to know - but not everything. To tell him the truth of it would guarantee disbelief and he would no doubt think she was crazy.

"So, let me see if I understand you correctly," he began. "Anne is the leader of some weird little cult and they intend to sacrifice me to their goddess?" At first, it was clear he definitely didn't

Christy Lynn

believe her, and she couldn't blame him. But, as he sat quietly for a few moments as Brigid just looked at him, he started to turn pale.

"Yes, that's basically it," Brigid replied, turning to look out the window. She had this feeling that if she looked him in the eyes, he would know she was partially lying and holding something back. "But they're not some weird little cult, Den. Don't underestimate them. Look where they live, for god's sake. They're powerful killers with deep pockets."

"Figures," he breathed. She glanced back at him, her head tilting as if asking a question. "My sister back home told me if I moved something bad would happen. Damned, New York City," he chuckled, making an attempt at his usual humor, but the corners of his mouth quivered.

Brigid felt the overwhelming urge to climb onto his lap and cuddle against that wide chest. The feeling was strong enough to make her nervous, so she compromised by inching a bit closer and laying her hand on his thigh to appear she was only being sympathetic to the situation, when the truth was, she was dying to just touch him.

Again, that tingle of soft electricity.

"You're not from here? Where's home?" She was rather surprised Anne would consider sacrificing him, since he had family and people who would miss him. Then again, she probably

The Sacrifice

didn't bother qualifying him as a potential candidate. Anne had grown bolder through the ages, instead of more cautious. Her arrogance was causing her to make mistakes in several aspects of the coven's transactions and business.

Den looked at her hand on his leg. Her pearly skin was a startling contrast against the black, cotton lounging pants. With a soft smile, he enveloped her small hand with his large, rough one. "Front Royal, Virginia. It's not far from Washington, D.C."

"Oh, I've been there! What a lovely, little town," Brigid blurted, before thinking. She had to be careful giving too much information to this stranger. It would be hard to explain how she had traveled to nearly every small town in the United States, and almost every country in the world, with the exception of Finland; no particular reason for never going, just hadn't made it there yet.

"You've been there?" he leaned closer, keen interest swirling in his eyes.

"I, uh, spent a lot of time in Virginia years ago," she winced. Damn it, shut up, Brigid! she scolded herself.

"Oh, I see, visiting grandpa and grandma in the summers," his voice had lowered to nearly a whisper, the sexy baritone of it making her sex damp. Tenderly, he brushed one of those wispy strands from her face.

Christy Lynn

The air between them had suddenly changed to a strange intimacy. At times like this, she cursed what she was; she has never been able to know for sure if a man was truly interested in her, or simply answering the succubus's call to his primal, male needs. It was the main reason she never let herself fall in love, after from her first love, Colin McCarthy, when she was only sixteen years of age in her home country of Ireland;

"Something like that," she whispered back, her greenish-yellow eyes becoming glazed and her lids lazily closing halfway. "It's been a long day, mind if I just…" She nestled against him and tentatively rested her head on his shoulder.

Why was she suddenly so tired? Usually, if she touched someone, she became amped. A moment ago, she felt like the energizer bunny, now she felt like she was crashing from the effects of a triple shot of espresso. What was she doing putting her head on his chest? The muffled thumping of his heart was soothing, and, for the moment, she couldn't care less if she was acting appropriately or not. He wrapped his arm around her and pulled her tighter against his side. Gently, he smoothed her hair and petted her like a child. Yes, he was definitely a dominant, always poised to care for those around him.

Suddenly, she pushed away and stood. She was a Domme, not a little girl! She was a creature of time, a predator through the ages. She had no

The Sacrifice

need to seek the feeling of safety and protection in the arms of a man. She refused to look at him and promptly walked to the other side of the room. To his credit, Den let her go without question, giving her the space she obviously needed.

She was confused now more than ever. She came here to find answers and, instead, found more questions. There was something reserved and sad, perhaps even haunted, about Dennis Markham. As close as she was to him on that loveseat, a normal person would have attempted something sexual with her due to the constant production of succubus pheromones...but he just held her, as she needed.

Just then, the front door opened and closed with a loud bang! Brigid and Den both sprang to attention, ready to face whatever was coming. "I heard you were here." Barrex blew into the open living room like a flamboyant, spring breeze.

Brigid exhaled with relief. "Hey."

"Well, well, if it isn't the hottie from the club," Barrex whistled, letting his eyes slowly scan Den's body from head to toe; lingering a little too long near the waistline of the slouchy pajama pants.

Den extended his hand, grinning tentatively, as if embarrassed by Barrex's blatant inspection. "I'm Dennis Markham."

"Barrex Whelan, Brigid's brother." He shook Den's hand then turned to his sister. "And what do you think you're doing?"

Christy Lynn

"What?" Brigid shrugged.

"Uh huh, don't play stupid with me. What are you doing, Blue?" He folded his arms across his chest.

"You two obviously need to talk. I'm going to excuse myself and get dressed." Den slipped out of the room and disappeared down the hallway, while Brigid and Barrex continued to glare at one another.

"Don't do it, Blue," Barrex was the first to break the silence.

"Do what?" she snapped through clenched teeth. Something about Barrex's demeanor was making her instantly irritable. "I honestly don't know what you're talking about."

"Help him," Barrex tossed his head in the direction in which Den had disappeared. "It isn't worth it. He's just another human."

The thought hadn't crossed her mind, or had it? Barrex knew her better than she knew herself; no doubt he knew what she would do before she did. The tension dissolved from her body and she sank back down onto the loveseat.

"He's not just another human. I like him, Barry," she breathed, barely saying the words loud enough to be heard. "Very much."

The shock was crystal clear on her brother's face. Slowly, he lowered himself to the edge of the seat next to her. "Wow, can't say I saw that one coming." He stared at her, a slow wrinkling the crow's feet at the corners of his eyes. Absently, he rubbed his short, perfectly trimmed beard.

"Looks good on you," Brigid reached out and tugged on a short whisker.

"Yeah? Doesn't make me look too old?" They both chuckled, as if anything could make them look their true age. "So, you like him? Once again, wow." He kept looking at her with the strangest expression.

"What?" she snapped.

"I just can't believe it. I'm trying to remember when I heard you last declare such a thing, and I can't. You never even said you liked Gerald Truman on your wedding day. But you like this guy?"

"Shut up," she hissed, glancing quickly down the hallway to be sure Den hadn't overheard. "And I liked Gerald, but the marriage was for money, not love."

"Love? Oh, really?"

"No, that's not what I meant. I'm not saying I love this guy," Brigid's temper was starting to heat. She hated when Barrex teased her.

"Hey, you're the one that brought up that word, not me." He held his hands up, palms facing her in mock innocence.

He suddenly stood and headed toward the kitchen. "Well, what's the plan?" he called over his shoulder. Brigid heard the vacuum sound as he pulled open the refrigerator door.

Christy Lynn

"Get out of my kitchen! Every time you come to my house you raid the fridge. Shall I loan Layla to you, since your staff doesn't know how to go to the grocery store."

Barrex returned with two bottles of beer in hand. He fit one on the edge of the coffee table and gave the lid a hard smack to pop it open. Brigid's feral-like eyes narrowed, and her nostrils flared. "Oh, c'mon, you don't care about the furniture here. We'll probably donate it all to Goodwill when you sell."

She was about to ask him how the hell he had heard she was planning to sell the condo, considering she had only mentioned it casually to Marshall Murphy two hours prior, but this was the Tower and news traveled fast. A few moments later, Den rejoined them, finding a seat of his own and accepting a beer from Barrex's hospitality.

"I have no idea what the plan is," Brigid finally answered his question. "I didn't even know I was going to get him out of this."

CHAPTER 7

The three of them made their way to the master bedroom, closing the door firmly in their wake. The staff knew better than to interrupt Miss Whelan when that door was shut. Den hastily shoved the few clothing items he had with him into his duffle bag, which was mostly filled with bondage gear he might have used at the club the night before, had he been lucky.

"Ok, what now?" He slung the duffle over his shoulder and faced the pair.

"Mmm, he really is nice to look at, isn't he?" Barrex spoke to Brigid without taking his eyes off Den.

"I certainly think so," she replied, rubbing her lower lip with her index finger. There was a look in her eyes as if appraising a piece of fine art.

"Guys, c'mon, quit messing around," Den grinned and rolled his eyes.

"Something wrong with being objectified?" Brigid snickered. "This way," she tossed her head, signaling the men to follow.

She led them to her large, walk-in closet. Barrex paused at the door. "I love a good pair of stilettos as much as the next girl, but can't you change clothes later? It won't be long before Anne hears you haven't left the building yet and curiosity will have her down here looking for you."

Brigid ignored him, disappearing around the corner of the heavy, wooden shoe rack. The guys watched as the unit slid easily to the right, revealing a passageway behind it. "Are you kidding me?" The men burst out laughing at Brigid's secret agent architecture.

She put her finger to her lips, signaling for them to be quiet so Layla didn't hear, and waved frantically for them to follow. It wasn't that she was worried Layla would tell Anne if questioned, she just didn't want Layla to have to lie for them. The housekeeper was a loyal employee, one Brigid has given a lot of trust over the years; she would never want her in a compromising position.

"What's back here," Barrex inquired, turning on the flashlight in his cell phone to better see in the dark space.

"When the coven purchased the Tower years ago, I pulled the floor plans through public records. On our floor between both condos, there's about a four-foot space, probably to buffer noise. If we climb down these boards we'll find a service stairwell that takes us to the main floor undetected. There's an emergency exit door that leads to the alley."

They looked down...way down. It was a black void of nothingness as far as they could see. Barrex couldn't help himself and let a penny drop through the abyss. He gave a low whistle when it

The Sacrifice

took almost fifteen seconds for it to hit anything at all.

Den balanced himself on a support beam. "Is it really worth all this? Let's just walk out the front door. I doubt anyone would recognize me. That Anne lady brought me here late last night. No one was around."

Brigid and Barrex looked at one another. "Oh, you were seen, and yes, they will be watching for you. You have to trust us, you're in real danger," Brigid replied. She wanted to scold him about following a strange woman home from a club, but reminded herself he had been compelled and decided to spare him her jealous scolding.

"What's that?" Barrex pointed at a thin line of light peering through a crack on the opposite wall.

"It's your closet," Brigid answered.

"Really?" Barrex crawled toward it, fitting his fingertips into the lip of the crawlspace door.

"We don't have time for this," Brigid was becoming impatient.

"I want to see what Freak is doing," Barrex let his voice drop even lower as he crawled through the tight opening and into his bedroom closet.

"Who?"

"Some guy I picked up last night. He told me his name, but you know me, I don't remember."

Brigid and Den hunkered down, peering through the small hole, watching Barrex carefully stepping on the polished, wood floor, trying not to

Christy Lynn

step heavy on a board for fear it would make a noise. Their view was, of course, limited and they were surprised when Barrex apparently found the guy somewhere down the hall.

"Oh, hey! Where'd you come from? I was just being nosey, I swear it. I didn't take anything. You got nice stuff, man." Freak's high-pitched voice was nasal and crisp in the silence of the condo. Brigid made a face; the guy sounded annoying. If he was hers, she'd have to gag him so she wouldn't have to listen to his voice. What had Barrex been thinking when he brought this one home?

So, he'd caught the asshole snooping through his drawers. This was getting good! Brigid and Den grinned mischievously at one another and quietly agreed to get a better look. Like soldiers under heavy fire, they belly crawled until they were able to see better through the closet door.

Waiting for Barrex was turning out to be awkward. Den was pressed against Brigid's side in order to see more, and the feel of his subtle body heat had every ounce of her attention. She was hyperaware of any movement he was making; even the expanding and contracting of his ribcage as he drew breath.

She was lying on several pairs of Italian leather shoes, discarded on the floor without care to place them in their proper cubbies. They were digging mercilessly into her stomach, yet, she would rather die a slow death by loafers than

The Sacrifice

move even an inch away from Dennis Markham.

"You ain't mad? Don't be mad, please? I like you, ya know? You're a cool dude. Don't want you having the wrong impression of me." They could hear Freak whining as he headed back in the direction of the master suite, no doubt chasing after Barrex. The two men came into view and Brigid could instantly tell something was wrong with her brother. She knew that look. He was his most quiet when he was his most angry.

Freak hurried his pace to get in front of Barrex, stopping and dropping to his knees. "I mean it, man, I was only admiring your watch collection. You have true style."

It was then that Brigid figured out the problem. Barrex caught Freak in his office. He had a rare watch collection in a glass display in that room.

"Do I?" Barrex tilted his head, his scowl softening just a trace.

Brigid saw his jaw muscle flex. He appeared to be deciding something. She didn't like this. Barrex was the most happy, playful, easy-going person she had ever known, but he had a temper that was dangerous in its swift judgment.

Freak was suddenly delighted when Barrex offered a hand in order to help him to his feet. "I know I sound like a broken record, but you ain't mad, right? I mean, I don't want nothin' to spoil the great night we had together." He paused and tried to be a little flirty in his demeanor. "I'm hoping there's a lot more nights like that to come."

Barrex smiled a soft, crooked smile and gently ran his index finger down the stranger's neck. "Shut up and kiss me."

Brigid froze; she may have even stopped breathing altogether. Surely, he was not going to do it, not now - not with Den watching! Horrified, all she could do was be a spectator as the one-night stand Barrex nicknamed 'Freak' let down his guard and eagerly rose on his tiptoes to reach Barrex's mouth.

In a matter of seconds, the scene ignited into hot passion. Freak seemed determined to make amends physically, using his body, alone. His lips touched every part of exposed skin, while his hands touched every part of covered skin. Through the layers of denim and cotton, Freak's small hand found Barrex's semi-erect member and began rubbing slowly.

Brigid was a true voyeur and not much turned her on faster than watching two people in the throes of passion...if only it wasn't her brother. However, with Den's body pressed against hers, every muscle in her body tensed, wanting to be touched in that way. Barrex buried his hands in Freak's tousled, sandy-colored hair, holding his head still as his eyes closed and his neck bent slightly forward. Their lips met and, in that moment, Brigid and Den both held their breaths,

The Sacrifice

so aroused with excited anticipation.

Please, don't do it, Barry, Brigid silently prayed.

She winced, biting her lip when she noticed Freak's knees weaken and eventually buckle. Barrex's biceps were straining through his button-down shirt under the weight of his victim's body. He didn't want Freak to fall...he wasn't finished. A few more moments, and Barrex finally let go, the corpse making a dull thud on the Berber carpet.

Remembering Den beside her, Brigid quickly looked at him. Was he alright? She caught the strangest expression on his face, certainly not the expression she had expected to see; then again, she wasn't sure what she expected to see. He did, of course, look shocked. But more evident was the fact he seemed to be concentrating on the scene, as if putting together pieces of a puzzle.

"Is he dead?"

"Yes. You okay?" Brigid asked.

His crinkled brow immediately relaxed, and he gave her a gentle smile. "Are you?"

He rolled onto his side and placed a large palm on her upturned bottom. He gave one perfectly rounded cheek a firm squeeze, inhaling harshly as if fighting the urge to ravish her right there in the dark closet amongst the smell of dry-cleaning, leather, and cotton.

"I'm fine." She gave a pointed look over her

Christy Lynn

shoulder at the area he had boldly placed his hand.

"Well, then, shut up and kiss me," he said, a cocky grin stretching his mouth as he repeated the words Barrex had said to Freak.

She couldn't tell if he was just joking, or if he meant it. His hand was still on her ass, after all, but his tone was light and playful. She decided to laugh it off, grabbing his wrist and abruptly removing his hand from her body and deliberately placing it on the floor between them. Something was different about this man. He just witnessed a homicide but appeared almost turned on; something wasn't right at all.

The thought crossed Brigid's mind that perhaps Den was truly scared to death on the inside, but smart enough to play it cool in order to live through escaping the Tower. But, if so, why go the extra distance to flirt with her? A movement in her peripheral vision caught her attention, and she looked in time to see Barrex stuff his hand into the dead man's pants pocket, withdrawing a very expensive Chupardy watch.

"Can't stand a thief," he snapped, tossing the watch onto the bureau. "We ready?" Barrex stood in the closet doorway, his engaging charm and light humor sadly absent.

***

The Sacrifice

Forty-five minutes later, the sleek, electric blue, Audi sedan that Brigid found parked in a no-parking zone near a dumpster in the alley beside the Tower, abruptly stopped in front of her Fifth Avenue apartment building. The pudgy doorman, who had a not-so-secret crush on her, rushed to open the car door.

Barrex jumped out and bent at the waist to look in the passenger window. "You said it's in the hall closet, right? Give me five minutes. I'll be right back down." He whirled on his heel, his long legs covering the width of the sidewalk leading to the door in three strides.

As soon as he disappeared into the lobby, Brigid threw the car into drive and sped off. She glanced a couple times in the rearview mirror to be sure Barrex hadn't seen them leave, then, focused on the road ahead. She could feel Den staring at her, but forced herself not to look at him.

"What are you doing?" he finally asked. "Your brother was getting your, what did you call it, your emergency bag?"

Brigid had asked Barrex to run up to her apartment to get the suitcase she kept packed with all the necessities she would need in the event she had to get out of town fast, which happened more times than she cared to admit. Barrex kept one packed, as well. It was unfortunately necessary in their world.

Christy Lynn

"Barrex doesn't need to be any more involved in this than he already is," she replied bluntly, eyes straight ahead as she dodged through traffic at white-knuckle speed. "He can't know where we're going, Den. You have no idea what Anne would do to him if she sensed he knew more than he was willing to tell her."

Dennis stared at Brigid's profile. "That's truly admirable. I mean it. You love your brother and I admire anyone who protects family above all else." As they entered the expressway, he turned his gaze out the window and resigned to go along for the ride.

CHAPTER 8

By the time the sedan pulled onto a gravel, one-lane road branching off from the state route on which they'd been traveling, it was well past sunset. Den still wasn't entirely sure where they were, except to say they were somewhere in Upstate New York. He'd dozed off around five o'clock; a serious error when being taken to an undisclosed location by a strange woman, whose brother he'd just witness commit murder.

The narrow road they'd turned on was shrouded by heavy evergreens, and was probably better described as a lane, instead of a road."We're here," Brigid announced, her voice excited, yet oddly hushed.

"Where?" Den asked, leaning forward in attempt to see past the white illumination of the LED headlights.

After driving about a quarter of a mile further into the woods, a cabin came into view and Brigid threw the car in park. A heavy sigh escaped her lungs before she climbed out of the driver's seat. "About time! God, I hate driving," she grumbled, stretching her entire body in a feral sort of way. She caught Den's eyes on her from over the roof of the car and felt a warmth from the knowledge

Christy Lynn

he was watching her.

There was a key hidden under a good-size rock at the corner of the cabin and within minutes a soft, yellow glow spilled out of the front door onto the large porch. Brigid waited patiently for Den to come inside, amused as he hesitantly opened the screen door and visibly winced when it slammed shut behind him. She never replaced the original door because every show she ever watched on television had a screen door that slammed, pissing off the mother of the house. It's funny how such a noise always seems to irritate a person. She liked it.

He looked pleasantly surprised at the room in which he was standing; that look was all the compliment Brigid needed on her little log home sanctuary. It was something straight out of a Pottery Barn catalog; soft textures and natural surfaces of wood and stone. Faux fur rugs and overstuffed everything filled the large, open space. His eyes rolled upward toward the vaulted ceiling and Brigid saw him catch sight of her leaning on the railing of the loft, watching him pensively.

"This is beautiful," he smiled his approval.

Brigid liked how easy he was with compliments. He had a way of giving them without making a person feel strange receiving them, yet they were genuine. She folded her arms across her chest and let her eyes sweep the expanse of the place. "Thank you," was all she managed to say.

They spent what felt like hours keeping a wide, awkward berth around each other. If Den wandered into the small reading nook, Brigid moved to the living room. But, now that the adrenaline from their escape had worn off, their stomachs needed satisfied and they found themselves forced together in the rustic-chic kitchen. A succubus could not live by chi alone; their bodies being organic, just like a human's, needs vitamins and nutrients, as well.

Brigid explained she employed caretakers who kept the cabin stocked and ready. They had no problem finding the fixings to make double-stacked sandwiches; black forest ham, lettuce, Dijon mustard, and aged Swiss cheese. As the food absorbed into their systems, the tension mellowed and conversation began to flow. Sip after sip of Guinness dark draft began easing Brigid's defenses, and soon she and Den were chatting pleasantly.

"With a place like this, why live in the city?" Den tipped back his bottle for another swig.

Brigid looked around the room again, smiling to herself. "You're definitely a country boy, aren't you?" she giggled freely. "But it's a good question. It really has something, doesn't it?"

Truth was, she had often considered taking permanent residence here, but the thought of

Christy Lynn

anyone knowing about its existence put a sour feeling in her stomach. The cabin was more than a vacation home, she needed this refuge. It was her own, personal place on this earth that was hers, alone. Having been born in a time when life was far less complicated, and moved at a much slower pace, the need for solitude and peace had become more frequently urgent – and necessary - as the age of technology dawned, connecting the world in ways never before seen.

Keeping one's privacy had become a lost art, and now people shared everything online from what they had for breakfast to concerns about the color of their bowel movements. She knew firsthand the absolute bliss and peacefulness of being disconnected from social media and the world around her, and it saddened her that people of this era did not.

Den cleared their plates and rinsed them in the sink, casting glances at Brigid as she absently played with an empty bottle of beer. "Tell me about your tattoos." Brigid stopped twirling the glass bottle and rested her chin in her hand, giving Den her full attention in hopes he would actually discuss something private about himself.

Den's shoulders stiffened noticeably, and he kept his back turned on her, pretending to be busy with the running water in the sink. "Conversation for another time, alright?" he answered, quietly.

She picked up immediately that she had hit a

The Sacrifice

nerve, and not wanting to press and ruin the ease of their evening, she let the topic go without further prodding. "I've never brought anyone here before," she offered, thinking perhaps it would be better to keep the subject on her as the main focus, but suddenly found the spotlight a bit too bright.

"Not even Barrex?" Den gave her a teasing look of mock surprise.

She shook her head. "No, not even him. He doesn't even know it exists. I think everyone needs a place to hide from their lives on occasion."

"I agree, but most of us can't afford it, so we go to a Holiday Inn Express for a weekend."

Brigid chuckled sadly. "Unfortunately, when I need to hide, a weekend at a hotel just won't cut it...obviously." She gave him a playfully accusing glare.

Den raised his bottle in salute to her insinuation that he had complicated her life beyond her comfort zone. "Touché," he grinned that endearing smile she had already come to recognize and love. He meandered around the kitchen island and took a seat next to her.

She noticed again that single dimple in his right cheek. Playfully, she poked him with her index finger right in the adorable pit. "It's so cute you only have one dimple." Den grinned and rubbed his face where she had just touched, turning his head a little so Brigid couldn't tell it

Christy Lynn

embarrassed him slightly that she had noticed such a small detail.

"Oh my god, are you blushing?" Brigid laughed at him, punching him in the shoulder. "Well, big, bad Dennis Markham, pink is very becoming on you."

He shot her a look, but it quickly evaporated into a shy smile. "It's not a dimple," he confessed. "I was bitten by a dog when I as a kid. It's a scar."

"Scars are sexy," she looked at the small indent again, and saw the silvery-white puncture mark where it had grown back together with scar tissue. Her eyes roamed his face and she suddenly noticed several duplicate marks, just big enough to fit a tooth. He must have been mauled pretty badly.

A comfortable silence fell between them and they stared at one another for, what felt like eternity. Brigid was falling deep enough into Den's gaze she was able to truly admire the color of his eyes. She took another slow sip from her beer bottle, but didn't take her eyes off of his. Closer she peered, her head tilting to get a better look. She was intrigued to find they weren't just deep blue. They had black flecks scattered within the irises and a thin, aqua line surrounding the pupils. Beautiful. For a moment, she felt she could be content looking into them for the rest of her life.

Finally, Dennis leaned back in his chair, his

The Sacrifice

posture lazy and his bottle, which was empty, balanced on his knee. Those beautiful, blue eyes were suddenly looking a little glazed from the alcohol. He was staring back at Brigid and gave her that sexy grin that had melted her the night she first met him in the club. "What are you looking so intently at?" he asked.

Quickly, Brigid's eyelids fluttered as if snapping her out of a spell of some sort. She smacked the tabletop with both palms and prepared to stand. "Anyway, I hope you don't mind the couch. There's only one bedroom, you know."

She slid off her stool and hurried to the Far East India, seventeenth-century steamer trunk in front of the couch that doubled as a coffee table. She had actually used it as luggage once when she and Barrex sailed around the Cape of Good Hope, South Africa, while journeying from India back to England.

She swung open the large lid and pulled out a pillow and goose down comforter. Hastily, she tossed it on the couch and nearly jogged up the stairs to the loft, leaving Den staring, confused over her abrupt retreat. Why the sudden freeze?

***

There were no clocks in the cabin. Whenever Brigid was able to spend a few days of respite

Christy Lynn

here, the pressing weight of time was something she preferred not to have on her shoulders. Den touched the screen of his phone to bring it to life, squinting against the bright light. 2:15am, damn, he thought, huffing and falling back onto the pillow. He'd only been asleep an hour and a half but felt as refreshed as if he'd been knocked out for the entire night. Now, he was awake...too awake.

He suddenly remembered there was a small, aged book he saw tucked under a throw pillow in the reading nook. He'd wanted to look at it, but it was obvious by the way Brigid had shoved it under the large pillow when he entered the space, that she didn't even want him to see it, let alone read it.

Of course, the very fact she didn't want him looking at it made reading it a requirement, as far as he was concerned. One way or another, he was determined to learn all he could about that fascinating creature who was snoring like a bullfrog in the loft above.

Quietly, he crept across the living room floor and around the corner into the nook. The window seat was way too comfortable as he nestled onto it and pulled a throw fur across his lap, as he'd seen Brigid do. He reached above his head and clicked on a small reading lamp hanging on the wall.

The tiny sconce produced the perfect amount of light for the scant space and managed to keep

The Sacrifice

Dennis in the haze of drowsiness that always accompanies insomnia. He ran his hand under the throw pillows lining the long, bench-style built in until he felt the soft, velvety cover of the leather-bound book he was not supposed to see.

He pulled the book from its hiding place, only after double checking to be sure Brigid hadn't been awakened by his late-night snoop fest. A grinding sound, like someone gargling glass, echoed under the vaulted ceiling; she was still sleeping soundly. He was quite safe to continue.

Upon inspection, the book looked even older than he originally thought. The leather cover was cracked and peeling and bore dark areas where Brigid had obviously attempted to preserve it by rubbing it with some sort of oil or leather preserver. He took special care untying the strings that kept it closed, committing to memory exactly how it was knotted so he could repeat it before slipping it back under the third pillow where it had been stashed.

When he opened the cover, it made a crackling sound, like stepping on dried leaves during an October stroll. It gave him the impression the old literature was in the autumn of its life. Its apparent age immediately captured his curiosity and he hastily, but gently, flipped through the sepia pages.

It was handwritten, he hadn't expected that. Quickly, he scanned a few of the fanning pages for

Christy Lynn

entry dates, thinking perhaps it was a journal. In which case, he would put it back and not read it. He respected the private thoughts of others, no matter how tempting it was to read. But no dates were to be found.

Den wiggled his body against the larger pillows beneath the sconce light, carving a comfy niche to relax into as he began with page one.

My dearest twins from the Gods, the author began. The words were written in small, flowing letters that reminded Den of the examples of great works from the Elizabethan era he'd been made to study in his high school English class. I wish with all my being we had more time, but the Abbot will be here steadfastly to carry ye both to yer new lives as devotees of the Anglo-Saxon God. As I have assured ye previously, ye are not to despair over whether or not our own Gods will be angered by yer supposed conversion. Remember, ye are not converting to this strange, ruthless faith of Papist, but only finding respite from yer own people who wish to do ye harm. Our Gods know it is necessary for yer survival to hide away in Glenstal Abbey in the County Limerick.

I have so much to teach ye, but no time to do so. This time has dawned upon us too soon, my loves, but I shall share what I am able within these pages. Most assuredly, the most pressing instruction shall be of love; considering ye are both slaves to it. In this subject, I am most

The Sacrifice

learned.

Brigid, my beautiful, mournful daughter, ye must cease yer incessant sadness. A man shall not desire such a depressive attitude in a wife. Hold pleasing thoughts of days past, when ye playt happily with Barrex in the wildflower meadow near the fishing pond. Holding happy memories close shall aid ye in keeping a smile on yer lovely face. A smile will open many doors, when a frown will not.

My beloved Barrex, may the Gods save all women – and men, yes I know of yer innermost private desires, even if ye do not - from yer wicked charms! Ye possess the attractions and appearance of the God of war, who is yer namesake. Ye must keep this foremost in yer mind. Ye must not use the ladies to keep boredom at bay, they are not playthings. I pray ye never suffer a broken heart, but if ye do not take care, ye will break many.

Suddenly, Den heard a noise, like the creaking of a board under the weight of a step. He put his finger on the page he was currently reading and closed the book, ready to tuck it away, if need be. With alert ears, he listened for several moments, but no sounds followed the first, the house must just be settling.

So, he flipped the book back open and continued. He was thoroughly engrossed. This strange little book was clearly centuries old, yet

Christy Lynn

the author was speaking to people named Brigid and Barrex! This couldn't be a coincidence, surely. Unable to delay, his eyes resumed their fascinated reading.

Ye both know the consequences of physical pleasure for deities such as yerselves, yet, I am aware of yer needs. Ye must always exorcise extreme caution when choosing whom to prey upon. Study yer victim. Note upon whether the person is connected in family or parish. Ye do not want to deplete a person who shall be missed, in the event such person does not live through the coupling.

Den exhaled loudly. So enthralled in what he was reading, he hadn't realized he had been holding his breath. "What the fuck?" he murmured.

He let his eyes drift toward the stairs to the loft. From his vantage point, he could only see the first two steps, but in his mind's eye, he could see the mystery above snuggled under a fluffy, down comforter. What could the author of this apparent guide to survival mean when calling Barrex and Brigid deities?

For a few moments, he simply held the book open to the current page and chewed on the inside of his lip. What was all this talk of depleting victims and consequences of physical pleasure?

Ye both have experienced how deeply attached one may become upon receiving yer

The Sacrifice

kiss...be conscious of it. One in love may become obsessive, and obsession oft' times leads to investigation. Anonymity in such a small world is the absolute necessity of yer lives, my loves. Ye shall not survive without it.

I wish to emphasize at this moment, to maintain compassion for those on which ye prey. Do not allow yerselves to grow hard of heart and jaded against the concept of love. Ye may not think it now, but love is possible for those of yer kind. 'Tis true there are few others, in comparison to the mass of humans, however, ye only need one of yer kind to love.

Den sat up straighter. "One what?"he asked aloud. Quickly, he glanced toward the steps. He to be more careful. Thrilled to have this jewel of information in his hands, he buried his nose back in the pages.

Oh, my dears, I must forewarn ye. There are things ye must know if ye meet another and decide to mate. If ye take him to yer bed, know ye may set yerself a most painful situation. A succubus cannot be seduced by the green-eyed monster of jealousy. If ye mate with another succubus and do not couple with humans, ye shall drain one another until death is inevitable, having no resurgence of chi. Yer kind cannot replenish chi of yer own accord, and to steal it from another, such as yerselves, is like drinking from a riverbed during a drought.

Christy Lynn

Dennis quietly closed the leather book, pinching the bridge of his nose in thought. Not wanting to push his luck further and risk being caught, he clicked the reading lamp off and made way back to the couch, book still in hand. He decided to keep it, regardless the possible consequences if Brigid found out. It seemed somehow relevant to him, personally, and he needed to find out why.

CHAPTER 9

"The Tunisians have a saying," Brigid said. She took a seat on the stool at the kitchen island, amused to find Den attempting to make breakfast for her. Was anything more adorable than a man in the kitchen? Fortunately, he found toaster waffles in the freezer; couldn't screw that up too badly. "The pretty is in the morning. Meaning, if you really want to see if a woman is beautiful, look at her when she first wakes up," she pointed at her sleep-mussed hair and made a sour face.

"The Tunisians, eh?" Den chuckled and sat the butter and syrup in front of her. "I think there's truth to that. You should skip the makeup. Your natural look is gorgeous. I prefer it."

Brigid tucked her chin to hide the pleased smile that creased her cheeks. It was such a simple compliment, yet it carried a great impact. "So, what will we do today?" she asked, cheerfully. She always slept like a baby when at the cabin, and last night had been no exception.

Den leaned on the island, sipping a small glass of grapefruit juice. "Not sure. I have a new pair of restraints I wouldn't mind trying out." He gave her a mischievous smile and raised his brow as if asking if there was any interest.

Christy Lynn

To Den's complete surprise, Brigid smiled back; a surprisingly welcome smile that suggested there may, in fact, be an interest. "What sort of restraints?"

Den's dominant nature peered tentatively from behind its clever mask and his smile slowly faded. "Does it matter?" The deep, liquid quality of his voice jolted the very sensitive receptors throughout Brigid's body, and she felt a delicious tingle down her arms and back.

"I guess not," she tried to laugh, but it felt wrong, considering the sudden change in atmosphere.

She'd wanted nothing more since the moment she laid eyes on Dennis Markham, than to shag him mercilessly, so why had she been avoiding doing just that? Perhaps it was confusion? She couldn't figure out if she wanted to ride him until they were both black and blue, or if she wanted to give herself to him, submitting to please his every desire. For the moment, it appeared the decision was being made for her. Den had made it clear he would not bend to her will, and by inviting her to wear his bonds, he was inviting her to submit.

What started out as a teasing jest had quickly turned into serious reality, and suddenly, they found themselves considering morning sex.

"Do you need anything?" Den asked, pausing to check in with her before retrieving his duffle bag of tricks.

The Sacrifice

"I'd like to freshen up, you know, brush my teeth and wash my face." Brigid slipped from the stool and made way for the loft.

"I'm sorry, how thoughtless of me. Go ahead, I'll set up things down here." Den shook his head, frustrated with himself for being so hasty. He walked slowly to the living room to prepare for their scene.

***

Brigid's cell phone chimed, alerting her she had a text. Of course, a text would pop up at the exact moment she had soap in her eyes while washing her face. Quickly, she rinsed and wiped the residue with a towel.

You will find a blanket spread on the living room floor. Present yourself on it, naked, eyes on the floor. And you do not have permission to speak, the text said. You have ten minutes.

She smiled to herself - this was rather fun! She was always the one in control, setting every scene in her sex life, setting every scene in her business life, setting every scene in her life period. For this one day, perhaps she could let someone else set the scene.

Quickly, she put the phone on its charger by the bed and tossed the sexy, white lace peignoir back into the closet. Den had instructed her to be naked, so the garment wouldn't be needed this

Christy Lynn

time. She wasn't sure how she felt about being so vulnerable as to be naked and kneeling for inspection the very first time she was with him, usually she was wrapped in a tight leather dress, or corset - whip in hand. Lingerie and outfits were part of her kink, and without them, the experience would feel completely different.

Knock it off, Blue, she mentally scolded herself. Who's to say every encounter has to be in your comfort zone? Considering that just a few days ago she had been threatening succubus suicide in the form of starvation because she couldn't handle the mundane repetition of this life, or its consequences, change was not only good, but necessary.

Precisely eight minutes from receiving the text, Brigid was kneeling in the same, perfect posture she always required of her own submissives. Strange how completely exposed she felt with her knees spread to reveal her sex. Her hands were clasped behind her back, making her breasts jut forward, and she was sure to lock her gaze on the blanket beneath her. It was thrilling to finally experience what others she dominates feels; to be in their shoes, so to speak.

The sound of the bathroom door opening reached her ears and she subconsciously sat up straighter, fighting the urge to look up when she heard Den's feet on the wooden floor in front of her. The footsteps muffled when they stepped

The Sacrifice

onto the blanket and came into view. She felt a pang of excitement to see they were bare. He wore no shoes, which in her mind translated he was prepared for anything.

"Very nice," he said, matter-of-factly. She let her lips curl into a satisfied grin, oddly happy she met his approval. "Your safe word is...," he began.

"I don't need one," Brigid interrupted.

"You will if you interrupt me again," Den warned. Immediately, she tucked her chin and bit her lip. "Your safe word is red, easy enough. Is there anything you consider a hard limit? I'm asking a direct question, so you may respond."

Brigid took the opportunity to raise her head and give her neck muscles a rest. She closed her eyes a moment, thinking. She'd had centuries of learning her own body and pleasures, so turn-offs had already been determined long ago and never brought into the equation. "No animals and no fisting," she smiled, letting her eyelids part just a fraction to steal a glimpse of him.

He looked amazing! He was naked, except for a simple pair of black boxer briefs – darn, still no glimpse of his endowment. He'd taken good care of his body but wasn't a slave to the gym. She was happy to see a slight softness in the middle; she liked a little pudge on her men, gives a girl something to rub herself on. Long thigh muscles flexed invitingly and she ached to touch them. She felt a stirring between her legs at the thought of

Christy Lynn

the powerful thrusting in which those thighs could assist.

Den smiled at her response. "Eyes on the floor," he casually reminded her. "No animals, no fisting, got it. Anything else?"

"Anal play. Normally, I wouldn't mind, but it's too early in the day." Her cheeks flushed red, hoping he wouldn't dwell on her meaning.

"Dually noted." Den stepped closer to her kneeling form. "Crawl over here and say hello."

Brigid wasn't sure what he meant by that, so she did exactly as commanded. She gracefully slinked her way toward him, like the feral cat her eyes resembled. When she reached the tip of his toes, she looked up at him, smiled cheerfully, and said, "hello."

Den burst out laughing. "Ok, I can see I'll have to be more precise. Greet me in your favorite, submissive way."

"I'm sorry, Sir, I know I'm not supposed to talk, but I don't have a favorite way. I've never done this before." She felt awkward suddenly and wanted to go upstairs to her loft and forget the whole thing.

Barrex had once said he always loved her need for perfection, but at times it could be self-defeating. This was one of those times. Without exact instruction, she had no idea how Den wanted her to perform and it was making her angsty. Brigid was an overachiever, the type of

The Sacrifice

person that won't try something unless they know they will excel at it. Being a submissive leaves too much gray area and she doesn't like the unknown.

"Oh. I see," Den said, reaching for her hands to help her to her feet. "I know you'll probably punch me for being sexist, but I just assumed that being a woman, you had, at some point, submitted."

Brigid put her hands on her hips and gave him the look, which made him laugh again. "I know, I know," he chuckled. "What do you need from me to help you?"

She was pleasantly surprised he asked. "Direction," she stated simply.

Den nodded, watching her closely. "Easy enough."

As they stood there, his eyes began to roam her body. Brigid saw his cock swelling against the supportive cotton of his briefs and she wanted to forget the whole scene and just tackle him on the blanket. There is much to be said about good old-fashioned fucking.

Speaking of good old-fashioned fucking, earlier, when Brigid was brushing her teeth, she dealt with the dilemma of possibly draining Den to death during the scene. But she was still adequately satisfied from her threesome several nights ago and, as long as she made Den take frequent breaks, he should survive the act just fine.

Christy Lynn

Brigid was about to suggest they simply have sex without all the ritual of a full-on dominant/submissive scene, when Den's easy manner shifted, and she felt the atmosphere around them intensify. "Kneel," he commanded, just as he did that night in the club.

This time she didn't hesitate; she dropped to her knees and resumed posture. He stepped close to her, very close. She shivered when his fingers slid through her hair, starting at the scalp and gliding to the ends. Lightly, the strands flitted against her shoulders and back as they gently fell from his fingers, like droplets of soft rain.

With her eyes glued to the floor, every touch, every movement, was heightened. She was so aware of his body; so close to hers she could feel the tension vibrating in his muscles. Suddenly, he walked away. She couldn't help it, she broke command and cut her eyes in a sideways glance in order to watch him.

He opened the front door and window, letting the fresh, mountain air meander its way gently through the cabin. The smile that stretched her lips was one of appreciation; how did he know the aroma of pine mixed with the smell of the cabin logs warming in the morning sun would soothe her in a way nothing else could in that moment? The tension in her shoulders waned and she inhaled a long, relaxing breath.

Then, Den tossed his duffle bag onto the

couch, its contents clanking together, making Brigid's belly swirl with excitement. He fished through it, turning once to see if she was holding posture and keeping her eyes on the floor. She wasn't.

"Tsk! Tsk!" he clucked. "What a pity we have to pause our fun for a punishment. Why can't the naughty, little minx do as she's told?"

Quickly, her eyes resumed their forward position, but it was too late. "Come here, little minx," Den ordered. When Brigid hesitated, he added, "stand and walk here."

Brigid did as she was told, keeping her gaze downward. She stood in front of him, feeling like a girl who was in trouble in the principal's office. Den reached into his duffle and withdrew a tightly coiled, brown leather belt, rolled perfectly. He held the brass buckle and let the strap unfurl. Brigid saw the length of it as it unrolled in her scope of view, swinging menacingly.

He stepped behind her, and she jumped when he placed the palm of his hand on the curve of her right buttock. "Easy," he breathed in her ear. Slowly, gently, he let his hand glide along the smooth contour of her ass.

His heat warmed her back when he pressed his body against the length of hers. He squeezed her firm bottom and reached around her waist with his other hand, the belt still in his grasp. He used the worn leather like a feather, letting it

Christy Lynn

lightly tickle her torso from sternum to belly button. It dropped lower, slipping over her pelvic bone and brushing the flesh just above her clitoris. She thrust her hips forward in attempt to make the belt touch the small knot of nerves, but the attempt was futile, the strap moved with her body, elusive.

Den let it brush against her thighs and her sensitive knees, then pulled it quickly back up the length of her entire body and over her shoulder. The edge cut against her neck, burning a thin, red line into the tender skin. She swallowed hard, already so aroused she wanted to bury her fingers in her folds and bring herself to climax. But she kept her arms firmly at her sides, curious to see what he would do next; she could already tell he was a good dominant, who knew what he was doing.

"Can you feel my cock touching your ass?" he whispered.

She nodded.

Suddenly, she gasped in shock from a sharp pain! He smacked her buttock hard with his bare hand. "I asked you a question," he growled against her neck, his lips brushing that thin, burning line from the strap.

"I'm sorry, Sir," Brigid was amazed she was clear headed enough to think to apologize for her breech in etiquette. "Yes, I can feel your cock against me, Sir." She was sure to end every

The Sacrifice

sentence with Sir, since she required all her subs to address her constantly as Mistress when in her service.

Den pressed his hard shaft against the stinging butt cheek in the exact place he had swatted it. But his cock was hot to the touch, offering no relief from the handprint beginning to burn bright red against her white skin. She arched her back against him. He allowed the movement without repercussion.

"Bend and place your hands flat on the table," he said, pointing at the coffee table trunk. The feeling of the cool wood against her heated palms was a blessing. She rested her weight on them, letting her back arch downward to stretch her already aching muscles...god, she was out of shape!

Den moved her ankles apart, using his foot. She was utterly exposed in this position, bottom higher than her head as the coffee table was low to the floor. She knew he must be looking at her...all of her. She fought not to jump when his fingers unexpectedly grazed her wet slit. They ran from her clitoris, along her aching entrance while gathering lubrication on the fingertips, then onward to the entrance of her anus. As soon as he touched the tightly puckered hole, she stiffened, almost standing upright.

"I know your limits, little minx," Den purred. "Trust me."

Christy Lynn

Trust me. The words echoed in her ears.

Could she?

Timidly, she relaxed and allowed his exploration to continue. His slickened fingers slid onward, past the 'forbidden zone' and up the valley between her buttocks, until they came to rest at the base of her spine.

He gripped her hips with both hands firmly, digging his fingers into the soft flesh surrounding the sharp, protruding bones. He pressed his pelvis hard against her and she felt the tip of his cock straining to enter her swelling sex. Without even realizing it, she rose a little on her toes, trying to give it easier entrance. The tip, just the tip, slipped in and she instinctively pushed back in attempt to encompass it.

Den gripped her hips so hard she knew there would be bruises, and she could literally feel the fight ensuing within him. All it would take was one quick thrust...but, suddenly, he was gone. Her body swayed from the abrupt absence of him, but she held her position, not having permission to do otherwise. He wasn't gone long, presumably so he could get control of himself once again. Moments later, Brigid heard the leather strap slide through Den's hands.

"You have a beautiful pussy, but surely, you didn't think it would make me forget your punishment?" he teased. "Brace yourself, little minx."

The Sacrifice

Brigid pressed down on her palms and dug her toes into the thick area rug.

The first lash wasn't so bad. It stung a little, making the point of impact warm. He repeated the same, light intensity until her entire backside felt fuzzy and turned soft pink. The strap peppered the backs of her thighs, preparing them, as well. Den flicked the belt and it landed neatly between her legs, lapping against her swollen labia. She moved her thighs further apart and he did it again. A soft moan escaped her.

"Mmm, so needy," he murmured. "You're being punished to teach you to listen to your Sir's commands. Is that clear?"

"Yes, Sir," Brigid immediately answered. She knew what he was feeling in this moment, it was one of her favorite things; standing there, a body posed for use, permission to do anything that pleased her. She wondered if he found the sight of strap marks as they darkened across plains of flesh as erotic as she did. She wondered...thwack!

She yelped, knees bending against the sharp smack of the belt, and she quickly stopped wondering further about anything. Before she could catch her breath, another swat found its mark, causing her eyes to mist. A brief thought of amazement at the level of pain her submissives could take flashed through her mind.

The sound of the brass buckle falling to the floor reached her and she sighed in relief. Den's

Christy Lynn

hands found her waist and stood her upright. "Good girl," he whispered into her hair, as he drew her against his chest.

Brigid leaned into the embrace, suddenly needful of the security it offered. She inhaled his smell, stronger now as his arousal was beginning to simmer. Tentatively, she wound her arms around his torso. With Den, it seemed everything meant so much more, even something as trivial as a hug. At that moment, it meant to her complete acceptance.

His solid hands on her back, rubbing and soothing her, made the stinging of her backside more pleasurable than she could have ever imagined. She was suddenly glad he had spanked her, so she could experience this type of intimacy. Her eyes were closed, enjoying the feel of his body, instead of just the sight of it, and she kissed his sternum lightly with exploring lips.

His cock pulsed slightly where it was pressed against her belly, and a small drop of wetness smeared across her abdomen when she leaned to look at it. She had the overwhelming urge to touch every inch of him, to examine all the secret places only brought to light for those special enough to share with. Would he let her?

Questioningly, Brigid looked up at Den and caught his face unguarded. There was the briefest moment, before he realized she was looking, that she saw him. His eyes were closed, and his brow

The Sacrifice

crunched together in either sadness or love; both so similar when physically manifested. Love? Seeing it in him made it blossom in her, and she felt the sting of tears on her lids.

He looked at her upturned face in such a frighteningly tender way, she tried to pull back, but he tightened his grip around her waist and held her firmly in place against him. Their eyes were locked, searching for something, and Brigid had no idea what they would find. She let her fingers trail down his back, as he gently brushed the dampness from the crease of her left eye with his thumb.

His smooth skin turned into Braille as her light touch tickled him pleasurably, giving him goose bumps. She felt the slope of his ass and couldn't resist the opportunity to squeeze a plump cheek. Finding no protest to her exploration, she raised her mouth to his right nipple and blew a moist, warm breath across it, barely traceable. The nipple hardened, inviting the caress of her tongue. She sealed her lips around it, sucking lightly, pulling at it with her teeth.

He drew a quick breath, burying his left hand in her hair while keeping her pressed tight against him with the right. Brigid sucked harder and felt the telltale twitch of his cock in response. She smiled to herself, loving that moment of discovering a new erogenous zone.

Suddenly, Den grabbed her face in both hands

Christy Lynn

and brought his mouth down on hers. He didn't force her lips open with his tongue, which made her want it even more. Instead, he teased her, licking and nibbling the expanse of her mouth. She whimpered, wanting him to kiss her hard; to take her now!

He seemed to know her need, for he pulled her with him to the blanket, her body pinned beneath his weight. He was stretched along the length of her, perfectly positioned between her spread thighs. His hard cock was straining between them, the head rubbing her swollen clitoris. She loved that and pushed her hips upward for more friction. He worked his pelvis, pulling his long shaft back and forth over the small, sensitive nodule.

Already so near her climax, Brigid wrapped her legs around Den's waist and rocked in time with his movements. Finally, he pulled back far enough the head of his cock slipped along her soaked folds. He pushed himself up on his hands and looked down at her, writhing beneath him, trying desperately to somehow make his rock-hard member slip inside her.

"No, I can't," Den barely mouthed the words. She wasn't sure what he meant and didn't care - all she wanted was to fuck him now!

He bent once more to kiss her. When she felt his tongue against hers, her whole body rose in response. Her back arched upward, making her breasts ache to be touched. Den dipped his head, taking a nipple in his mouth. He sucked hard, making Brigid cry out softly. She grabbed for his hips, trying to push him inside her.

His mouth abandoned her nipples, leaving them cold in the mountain breeze still blowing through the windows. She opened her eyes to see the look in his, and for a moment was frightened. There was something dangerous stirring, mixing with the stormy blue of his irises as his gaze seemed to devour her.

Why she felt afraid, she had no idea. She should have been aroused, encouraging him, but she was not the one in control. She was the submissive at the mercy of this dominant, and the unknown was terrifying.

Frantically, she searched for something to lighten the moment. "Where are those restraints?" she chirped, smiling broadly in attempt to ease his intensity.

He grabbed her wrists, yanking her hands from his sides and pinning them above her head. "Fuck the restraints!"

She gasped as he suddenly thrust his large, hard cock deep inside her. Her legs fell from his waist, trying to accommodate his size. Farther, her thighs fell open. "God!" he growled, burying his head into her shoulder with his next thrust.

He tilted his hips just so, and Brigid saw stars. "Holy fuck!" she panted, trying to smash herself against him. More, she needed more! She strained against him, blind to anything but his body.

He held her wrists so tight, they were losing feeling and with his other hand he grabbed her throat. She swallowed reflexively against his palm and he squeezed tighter. "Look at me," he ordered, his cock vibrating inside her as he stopped pumping and held it still.

She met his terrifying eyes again, and this time saw only desire. "Are you alright?" He gasped. Whatever struggle was ensuing inside him, it was a battle that was leaving him winded. He kissed her, softly, trying to slow down. Brigid wasn't ready for soft. She bit down hard on his lip and bucked her hips against him.

She suddenly wished she hadn't pushed him, forgetting her place as his submissive. His hands slipped underneath her back and he lifted her, giving him unencumbered access. She shook, her breaths coming in short pants. He rammed her, over and over, and they fell back to the floor. He dug his knees into the blanket to give more thrust, pushing mercilessly deeper until she felt the pounding of his balls. Still, he worked, trying to get deeper, blindly boring into her depths.

Brigid was frantic in her desire. His grip on her wrists forgotten, she yanked them free and wrapped around him; grabbing, pulling, reaching for anything to hold onto; anything to help keep her from losing control. Her body was screaming, surging with him.

He fought her, capturing her hands and pinning her once again. "Hold still!" he threatened. His grip tightened to the point of bruising the tender, white flesh on the underside of her arms.

She was shaking her head, fighting against release. She never let herself go like this. Sex was for survival, having lost its pleasure and mystery eons ago. He had her immobilized and all she could do was lay there and take the ruthless pounding. With each stroke, the top of his shaft pressed against that elusive spot deep within, bringing her closer to the edge. Harder and harder he thrust. She fought to move, a futile act, he was too strong.

"Stop!" she cried suddenly. "I can't...." Why was she becoming so tired? Why wasn't he becoming tired? How could she not feel the rush of his chi filling her veins?

She hadn't used her safe word, so Den covered her mouth with his, silencing her words and fucking her harder, their bodies becoming slick with sweat. He hooked her leg behind the knee with his forearm and pulled it upward, opening her even further than she thought possible. She gasped, almost crying out again. "Let go, Brig, do it!" he panted between gritted teeth.

How did he know? How did he know she was wrestling with just that? He was a dominant, as

Christy Lynn

well, perhaps losing control was his struggle, too? Den pushed deep and stayed there, suddenly working his hips in a circle, grinding against her. That was it, the turning point. She'd never felt anything like it, and at that moment, she no longer cared about anything; not what she looked like, the words coming out of her mouth, the sounds forced from her throat with each milling of his hips.

He mercilessly ground her, taking her breath completely. "I'm not stopping. You'll come for me," he said.

Tears slid from the corners of her eyes as she squeezed them shut, needing to hide from the absolute exposure of the moment. Den kept himself buried in her, biting her jaw and the outline of her breasts; never breaking rhythm. Over and over he bore into her, her juices coating them both.

It started deep in her abdomen and began to build. Her breath caught in her throat as the blood rushed to her face. "That's it, that's my girl. Come for me, little minx." Den's mouth sealed itself in the curve of her neck, and he bit down – hard! Brigid moaned. Then, without warning, it happened like a blinding flash. Just as she was about to explode, she felt Den's hot release surge inside her.

"Oh, my fucking god!" she screamed, and her orgasm detonated deep inside her. It washed over

The Sacrifice

her in an intensity she had never felt in all her centuries. His semen released in her again and again in time with the waves of her own ecstasy. She felt it – everywhere - running into the crack of her ass, smearing her thighs, his belly, but he didn't stop.

Finally, she pushed against him one last time. "Please stop," she laughed and cried at once. "Red!"

CHAPTER 10

After her shower, Brigid found Dennis sitting quietly on the front porch. He hadn't heard her push the screen door open, and she stood silently watching him. He had the strangest expression on his face. Suddenly, his gaze dropped from the forest beyond to his lap and he shook his head. It looked like he was trying to come to grips with something.

Brigid stepped out onto the porch and let the screen door bang behind her to alert him of her presence. "That's an awfully serious look you have there," she teased. Slowly, she took a seat next to him, not liking that she felt the need to tread lightly after just having amazing sex with this man. "Can you share what you're thinking? I'd like to know." She watched his blue eyes closely.

He seemed nervous; fidgeting and exhaling an irritable breath. "How are you feeling, Brigid?"

The question surprised her. Why was he asking? Did he not enjoy what had just happened? "I feel wonderful, a little tired maybe...," she stopped in mid-sentence, realizing that what she said was very true. She was borderline exhausted. Why?

Dennis reached for her hand. He held onto it like it was the most precious thing on the planet.

The Sacrifice

"I want to tell you, but I'm afraid it might scare you. Please, don't leave. You need to hear what I have to say."

Brigid's brow wrinkled in concern. This man really had something serious hanging over him. "Oookay," she breathed.

"Look, Brigid, to be blunt, I don't usually penetrate a woman during sex. Or if I do, it's only for a few strokes. I prefer the kink of BDSM because it doesn't require intercourse."

Her eyes widened. Of all the things he could have said in that moment, this was the last thing she would have guessed would come out of his mouth. "I see, I think," she said. "I'm sorry if I pushed you too far. You're probably in Alcoholics Anonymous and one of the steps is to deny yourself a physical relationship for at least a year."

He shook his head and snickered. "You're smarter than that. You've watched me drink several beers since I've known you."

"Then why on earth would you deny yourself the puss?" Brigid looked at him with the same sour face she might've made had she eaten a lemon.

He paused, looking at her evenly. "I'm trying to tell you."

Quickly, Brigid clamped her mouth shut and pretended she was locking her lips closed with an invisible key, which she tossed over her shoulder. Den obviously needed time and she had to be

Christy Lynn

patient enough to give it to him. She looked again at the tattoo on his wrist; sexy, yet sad, in its design. Perhaps a change in subject would help him open up a little later?

"May I ask, did you get that tattoo in prison?" It was a difficult topic to address, considering he had already shut it down once before.

A deep gloom shadowed his handsome face and his blue eyes suddenly looked almost black. He pulled her to her feet and she followed him back inside, where he lowered himself onto the blanket, pulling her with him.

"Yes, I got it in prison. And yes, I did time. Not long, three months while the powers-that-be tried to decide if they could hold me longer while trying to build a homicide case. I didn't balk while they kept me, even though any attorney could've got me out on bail, all things considered. But, in truth, I wanted to be behind bars. Hell, I was hoping they'd find a way to give me a life's sentence," he murmured the last.

Brigid moved closer, nestling into that sweet spot just under a man's shoulder where a woman can feel small and protected, and a man can feel strong and protective. Den reacted as she had hoped, draping his left arm around her and pulling her against his chest.

"If you don't want to talk about this right now, you don't have to," Brigid offered him the exit she thought he might need.

The Sacrifice

"No, it's ok. I believe you may be the only person I know who might understand."

Suddenly, Dennis withdrew the small, leather-bound book he'd taken from its hiding place in the reading nook. Brigid's eyes turned a dangerous yellow and she pulled away from him, her back stiff as a board. "Where did you get that?"

"I saw you stuff it under the pillows in the nook. I couldn't help myself, and I'm glad I couldn't. I haven't read it all, but I swear, what I have read...Brigid, it means something to me."

Brigid snatched the book from his grasp and jumped to her feet. "It doesn't mean a damned thing to you, Dennis Markham! How could it? It was written for my brother and I by our mother!" She began to stomp out of the room, but Den's suddenly tortured voice stopped her.

"Listen! If I stick my cock in a woman, she DIES!" he yelled. "Do you hear me?"

Brigid stopped. She squeezed the book in her hands and drew a deep breath.

"This tattoo," he scrambled to his knees and held his forearm out for her to see. "It represents two women who have died because of...because of me. After what we just did, I don't know why you are still alive, don't you see?"

Helplessly, he sank back to the blanket on which they just had incredible sex. Brigid eyed him, so vulnerable, his soul stripped bare before

Christy Lynn

her. After another moment of indecision, she settled down, keeping a few of inches between them. She felt violated. He stole something incredibly personal, read it, and now thinks he can apply it to his own life. She needed him to explain his actions before she trusted him enough to nestle into that place of safety again. She felt very much the same as Barrex on the topic of stealing, and as far as she was concerned, Den was no better than Freak.

"Only two?" she asked after a few moments of silence.

"What?" he asked.

"You've only taken two lives?"

Den nodded. "When you say it, why does it sound like that isn't many?"

Brigid inhaled sharply. He had a point, she had better watch her mouth. But, in a moment of sympathy for Den's apparent state of misery, she decided to let him in. "It isn't many, Den. Not in comparison to the numbers I've accumulated over time."

She heard him take a sharp breath and saw a light of hope flicker in his eyes. Helpless against her ingrained, moral compass, she resigned to let her anger go and let him inside her world in order to help him.

"See? You can tell me anything," she laid her hand on his tattoo then let her fingers trail lightly down his forearm, all the way to the center of his

The Sacrifice

palm.

"Thank you," he began. "I was a kid, you know, first boners and all that. I was a sophomore in high school when I went to my first party. Of course, everyone was drinking and doing stupid shit. I had a thing for this girl, Missy Naylor, and she was there. We started fooling around and it went from first base straight to home plate." He covered one of the demons on his tattoo, leaving the second still exposed. "I discovered afterward, she'd been a virgin, too."

He fell silent so Brigid went to the kitchen. She poured two glasses of juice, being it was still early in the day, and settled back on the floor. She was parched after their scene, and figured he must be, too. Her hips were bothering her, but she didn't suggest they take this conversation to the couch; it felt too personal to move it from the blanket. The blanket, which moments earlier had served as an altar of lust, was now a safe place of confession.

"Rest in peace, Missy Naylor," she whispered, raising her juice in a toast to the young girl's soul. "And the other?" she glanced at the second demon.

"Obviously, the thing with Missy freaked me out. A young boy delirious in his first act of sex, only to realize after he pulled out and came all over the sheet, the girl wasn't breathing. So, I didn't date again...like ever. The doctors said Missy had heart failure. I tried to trick myself into believing that, but I knew better. Deep down I knew it was me...somehow." Dennis sipped his juice, giving Brigid a thankful look for pouring it.

"This one is Tamara Myers," he let his forefinger caress the second demon. "I was twenty-two years old. Tamara danced in a strip club. Her stage name was Ruby, which was funny because she was a blonde, not a redhead. Back then I frequented those type of clubs as a way of, well, at least some form of release and company. Like I said, I wouldn't let myself have intercourse, so I had to be creative. After months of paying her for lap dances, she decided I wasn't a total creeper and actually accepted my invitation to get Starbucks sometime. We hung out for a few weeks, until finally, she blew up on me. She was upset because I hadn't tried to fuck her and she wanted to know why. The accusations began...was I secretly married, or with someone else? Women in that line of work have a hard time relating to a man, unless it's sexual. I tried to tell her I did want her! She had the body of a pole dancer, so of course, I wanted to pound her senseless. Hell, I was bursting, and sick and tired of stroking off."

"Oh, I know that feeling," Brigid chuckled, managing not to allow any humor in the sound of it, because this was not a joke, by any means.

"One night, she came over, we turned on Netflix. Next thing I know, she's naked and my cock is in her mouth." Den started to look seriously uncomfortable. "She kept mentioning feeling so tired, all of a sudden. She apologized, making some excuse about dancing the dayshift earlier before coming over and the club had been unexpectedly packed for a Tuesday afternoon. I told her she should climb back up on the couch and watch the movie with me, but she seemed obsessed with the idea of touching me. I don't mean to sound arrogant," he blushed. "But all the women I've been with in my life seem to become just that...obsessed."

Brigid shook her head. "Trust me, you're not being arrogant. You're spot on, so far." She was beginning to suspect Den may be much more than either of them knew.

Den looked as though he was about to ask what she meant by that, but he continued his account of what happened, as if he were telling it again for the eighth time to the homicide detectives. "Finally, she laid back on the floor and begged me to take her. I did. Christ, I'm only human." He let his head fall into his hands.

"Well, no, I don't think you are only human," Brigid stated firmly. She took him by the wrists, staring point blank into his misting eyes. "I understand now why my mother's book connected with you. You're an Incubus, Dennis Markham."

"What? Wait. First off, you're being serious when you say it was your mother who wrote that book? How can that be? The person who wrote it references things from the Medieval Period. I figured you'd been named after the Brigid and Barrex referred to in those pages."

Brigid shook her head. "You're right, it was the Medieval Period, but it was our mother who wrote it. And she wrote it directly to Barrex and I. She was burned at the stake for witchcraft back home in Ireland when we were sixteen. Somehow, she knew her fate and so she wrote this while we were hiding in Glenstal Abbey, in hopes it would serve as a guide of sorts. She knew what we were, said we inherited it from our father. She was just a human woman." She fell silent to let the information sink in. "Dennis, who are your parents?"

He blinked, his brow crinkling in thought. "No one of consequence. I mean, they certainly weren't mythical creatures or something like that. Dad was an environmental engineer and mom was a florist. Why?"

"Because I just told you, you're an Incubus. Forgive me for asking, but is there any chance you were you adopted?"

That question hit him hard. She saw the sting of it flash across his face. "Yes." He took another drink of his juice and looked into Brigid's eyes for a long moment. "There was a discussion once when I was fifteen about the fact mom and dad adopted me...once."

The Sacrifice

"Well, one day you might want to find out who your birth parents are."

Brigid remained quiet, allowing Den to resume when he was ready. She did feel it was alright, finally, to touch him and the contact seemed to help them both as she wrapped her arms around his torso and snuggled against him.

"You're serious about this, aren't you?" he asked, his lips moving against the thick crown of her hair.

Brigid nodded. "You need to look at the evidence, Den. You think it's too farfetched, that there's no such thing as a succubus, but women die if you make love to them. Some would say that, in itself, is too farfetched." After a long silence she asked, "What happened to Tamara?"

"Again, the autopsy report stated heart failure. That's when I knew for certain it was me, not the untimely death of a young woman gone before her time. The police were convinced I'd murdered her. You know, the cliché of a patron obsessed over a dancer who killed her in a fit of jealousy." He shook his head and scowled. "I tried to lock myself away from the world..."

"To protect people from what you are," Brigid finished for him, knowing exactly what he was about to say.

"Yes." He looked so tortured. "I've been thinking, why am I here? I mean, in this cabin. Anne Fainn has no idea where I live. She doesn't

Christy Lynn

even know my real name." Den saw a strange look flit across Brigid's face, unaware she had let that important piece of information slip to Anne already. "Does she?"

Brigid rolled her eyes and sipped her water. "You really don't get it, do you? Trust me, by now they know who you are, where you live, and they've already been there."

"You're right, I really don't get it, and it's about time I learn the truth." Den gave Brigid a pointed look. "Come on, let's take a walk."

The Sacrifice

CHAPTER 11

The landscape in the bright sunlight was breathtaking; old, worn mountains blanketed with deciduous forests and wilderness as far as the eye could see. Pine needles crunched pleasantly underfoot as Brigid showed Den a small game trail not far from the cabin. It felt wonderful to be out of the house.

Before they got too far on their hike, Brigid pulled out her phone and sent a text to the caretakers letting them know they could go in and clean. She'd left a grocery list on the counter so they could restock the refrigerator.

"The air is so clean here, I can't breathe," Den joked. "Reminds me of home."

"Maybe you should think about going back to Virginia," Brigid suggested, sad at the thought of Den leaving, but knowing he would be much safer if he did. "Why did you move to New York, anyway?"

He stopped in the middle of the trail and Brigid almost crashed into him. "Go back to Front Royal, after the conversation we just had?"

Suddenly, before she could register what was happening, Den had both of her arms pinned behind her back. He yanked her toward a birch tree, pushed her backside against the smooth trunk, and handcuffed her around it! "What are you doing?" she demanded.

"The new restraints I wanted to try," he grinned. "New pair of handcuffs," he dangled the key between his forefinger and thumb, taunting her.

Casually, he took a seat on a log and laced his fingers together as if deciding on where to begin his interrogation. He cocked his head to the side, staring evenly at her as she thrashed and kicked at the piles of leaves around the base of the tree, accumulated over decades of Septembers.

"Who are you?" he asked. "No, who are you, really?" He interrupted when she opened her mouth to spit curses at him.

She went suddenly still, astonishment widening her eyes. "What do you mean?" she asked slowly. "You know who I am."

"Tell me you don't feel the electricity between us." He made a funny face and chuckled. "That sounds like a cheesy pick-up line, but I mean it literally. There's a physical reaction that happens each time we touch. You want me to believe it's because I'm an incubus, right?"

Brigid scowled and shook her head. After the hours she just spent trying to make him see the possibility he was something different in this world of humans, he still seemed as shut off to the idea as before. "You know what, Den, I don't care. Believe what you want. I don't mind helping you

The Sacrifice

connect the dots of your mystery in order to find out the truth, but it's obvious you're not interested in exploring real possibilities."

He stood, brushing bits of bark off his butt from the log and approached her, stopping only inches from her bound body. Gently, he stroked the side of her cheek, both of them shivering from the small surge generated by the caress. Suddenly, he fisted her hair and brought his mouth down on hers in a consuming kiss.

Instinctively, Brigid's eyelids closed and her head fell back to receive him. The sharp tang of pine resin hanging heavy in the air was overpowered by his masculine, unique scent and Brigid was suddenly grateful she was pinned against the tree, because her knees were failing her.

All of a sudden, something happened between them. The deeper they fell into their kiss, the intensity of the transference of energy between them increased to the point Den had to tear himself away. Brigid's heart was pounding in her ears and she was gasping for air. Her head felt light, as if filled with helium. She was overcome with an elation she never once experienced when decrementing chi from anyone in the past. Was this what the precursor to death felt like? Had they depleted the energy stored between them and was now tapping their own precious reserves?

Den leaned against her, his lips brushing her

Christy Lynn

ear. "I want you," he breathed. His forefinger trailed down her throat. "I want you more than anything I've ever wanted in my entire life." The words rang determined and true.

"You want me again so soon? I'm still sated from earlier," she lied. The familiar angst of arousal and hunger was clenching her stomach and sent a tingle down her spine; she wanted him just as badly. He slipped his hand under her sweatshirt, his fingers tickling her abdomen as they journeyed toward her breasts.

"Please, Den, I don't want anything to happen to you," she murmured into his mouth. "We tempted fate once already. I don't think we should do it again until we replenish our strength."

For some reason, her words stopped him cold. The sudden absence of his kiss made her open her eyes to find him staring into hers with a questioning look. "Why do you say that?"

The warmth of his palm on her belly warmed her and she knew she had to make this man believe the truth, because as much as she tried to ignore it, she was falling in love with him.

"You read Mother's book. She said if we ever met another succubus and fell in love, we had to be careful not to drain each other to the point of death. Do you recall reading that? Succubi need fresh chi, we don't produce our own. Understand?"

He touched the small indent above her nose, a

The Sacrifice

worry line chiseled out of years of the same expression. Softly, he stroked it, then placed a light kiss upon it. He drew back a little and gave her a lopsided grin. The grin clearly spoke of his disbelief in what she was trying to tell him.

"Damn it, Dennis, how many times do I need to repeat myself? You're an Incubus. I've told you that." As irritated as she was at him for being so stubborn - and apparently deaf - she felt an indescribable happiness at the realization that he was like her. If he was an Incubus, they could relieve their desires without the fear of killing one another...as long as they fed from humans when necessary.

"I didn't think you were being serious." Den gave her a sideways look. "You really are serious, aren't you? The two women," he glanced at the tattoo on his arm. "Are you saying they died because I'm an Incubus? I drained them of their life force?" He inhaled a breath so deep, his chest expanded, and he had to arch his back to receive it all. "Barrex is an Incubus, then. What he did to that man he called Freak, that's how it happened with Missy and Tamara - they quietly weakened and then slipped into a peaceful sleep."

"Well, that explains why you didn't panic when Barry drained Freak. I thought it was odd you took it so well." She felt her shoulders relax and she wished she wasn't cuffed so she could put her arms around him and comfort him again.

Christy Lynn

She remembered when she and Barrex learned the truth of their nature, it felt like a death sentence. Their mother had not been very compassionate in the telling of their fate. She simply said it, gave them a brief smile, then went to the kitchen to prepare dinner as if it were any normal day, as opposed to informing your son and daughter they were predators by nature.

"So, you are a succubus," he quietly stated, moving close to her again.

"Yes, now how about you uncuff me so we can go back to the cabin and figure all this out?"

He seemed to ignore her. "And when an incubus and a succubus fuck each other they don't have to worry about the other's safety?" Den's voice was adopting that low, raspy tone she noticed he got whenever he was turned on.

She smiled coyly. "Yes, and no. We drain each other of our natural energies, which is not necessarily a good thing, even though it feels amazing. We can drain each other to the point of death, if we aren't careful. Haven't you been listening at all to anything...," her mouth opened to say more and Den took the opportunity to fill it with his tongue.

His actions turned insistent, coaxing and needing. "You won't die?" he asked again while kissing her neck and pulling her shirt off her shoulder so he could nip her lightly with his teeth in that tender, delicious spot of sensitivity.

The Sacrifice

Brigid gasped from the pleasure of it. "Did I die an hour ago?" she nearly whined, her desire mounting with his. He shook his head. "No, Den, I won't die...so long as...," she didn't finish her thought, he didn't seem to be listening anyway.

A soft pressure between her legs made her spread her thighs, frustrated with the thickness of denim that kept her from feeling his touch as his thumb passed over the crotch of her jeans. He pushed her light pink sweatshirt up to her ribs, releasing her brazier with one hand from behind her back.

"Smooth, very smooth," she giggled at the move that all young men seem to learn by the time they graduate college.

He smiled down at her for a brief moment before taking her left nipple between his lips. Her back arched to press her breast further into his mouth, pushing her shoulders back against the tree trunk, the rough bark marking her flesh. Feverishly, he tore at the buttons of her button-fly jeans, yanking them down impatiently. She kicked one hiking shoe off and slipped her foot out of the pant leg, freeing herself from the restriction of pants around the ankles.

Den hooked an arm under her knee, pulling it up to her waist. Over the centuries, she has had sex in every imaginable position, but for some reason, the way Den held her, exposing her most intimate parts, the way he looked at her, as if he would stand there staring forever, made her feel more naked and desired than she could remember ever feeling.

With his free hand, he easily unhooked the button of his own fly and the loose pants fell in a pile at his feet. She let her gaze fall to see his erection as it sprang free from its cotton captor. Yes, he certainly had the characteristic trait of an incubus - large cock - and her inner-most depths clenched at the sight of his endowment. She felt an odd sense of ownership over it; this was her incubus and her cock to use for all eternity.

"Don't be gentle," she commanded, bracing herself for his assault.

"Don't top from the bottom, little minx," he snipped. "I'll tan your ass, if you do it again."

She opened her mouth to argue; she was a Domme, not a submissive, and he shouldn't expect otherwise. But his hand suddenly covered her mouth at the exact moment he thrust that huge cock inside her. She gasped behind his palm, eyes growing wide as he stretched her. Their eyes were locked, her cheeks flushing crimson from the exquisite violation.

Had anything ever felt so incredible? In that instant, her soul bound itself to his. An incubus and a succubus pairing was a powerful thing, a bond stronger than mortal marriage. Neither of them knew what they were creating as they surged toward their climaxes, not even Brigid. True, her

The Sacrifice

mother had written on the subject, but didn't go too far in detail. Perhaps, she never truly believed Brigid or Barrex would actually find another of their kind to love. It was just too rare an occurrence. Maybe it was a good thing she had not described the bonding, and all that it involved, because Brigid may have kept her heart securely under lock and key for eternity and missed the experience of love.

She was aware of nothing but him, nothing but Dennis Markham; his warmth, his smell, his soft, urgent breath on her neck, his hands on her hip and in her hair. Every cell in her body was charged by the chi that was her turn to steal. Now, she knew for certain her existence had a purpose other than misery; this was what it felt like to be a goddess! This would make immortality worth every agonizingly long hour.

He seemed to instinctively know her body, know every erogenous spot she possessed and was somehow able to touch them. He pressed his pelvis against her most sensitive knot and thrust over and over again. Tears were streaming down her face, mingling with a thin line of blood from her bitten lip; she bit it earlier that morning and now the wound was fresh again. He licked it, wanting to taste the coppery flavor uniquely her own. Even her blood tasted different; stronger, more metallic. His cock swelled larger, hard to the point of pain, and he needed to release himself inside her; to claim her.

Christy Lynn

"You are mine!" he snarled. He was not himself with her, but something bestial, primal. His momentum increased, propelling them both to a place neither had ever known. "Say it, Brigid! Say it!"

Her head was swimming dizzily. She couldn't get enough of him. Her arms burned from abrasions and she wanted to touch him so badly. She could feel the years of celibacy and restraint pouring from him into her, dissolving in her empty womb to never be felt again. The solid truth of his body against hers was the only truth that mattered.

As they mounted the summit and reached the crest of their pleasure, Brigid cried out "I'm yours, Dennis Markham! Yours!"

The Sacrifice

CHAPTER 12

The forest around them ignited into life. Birds were chattering in the canopy above, and squirrels sprang from branch to branch in their eternal game of chase, causing bits of bark and limbs to rain down on them like a World War II airstrike. Everything had changed somehow, leaving Brigid feeling unburdened and carefree in a way she could never remember feeling before.

She giggled easily when Den picked a torn bit of leaf from her hair, challenging any squirrel brave enough to fight him. "I'll protect you, my princess!" He playfully puffed up his chest and turned to face the invisible foe in the trees.

Brigid's left brow rose in admiration as she viewed his naked backside. A breeze stirred, making the pine trees hiss as it rushed through their thick, green branches. Goosebumps coated her arms and legs. "How about unlocking these things so I can get dressed? I have a lot to tell you and I'm sure you have a lot of questions." She glanced down at her nipples, which were pointing sharply. "A bit nippy today, isn't it?" she laughed, making a joke of her own in hopes of bringing that sweet smile to Den's face.

She realized she asked him twice already to

Christy Lynn

uncuff her. He seemed to like her restrained and she actually didn't mind it, either. Then it occurred to her, whenever she would bind a sub, the more they asked for something, the longer she'd make them wait for it. She had a bit of a sadistic side, and perhaps Den did, too.

She shook her head and tried to focus on something else. "What year were you born?"

He gave her a funny look. "You've noticed the gray?" He ran his hand through his hair, making it poof, as if he just removed a motorcycle helmet. "Let me guess, you don't like older men."

"Um, I wouldn't bet on you being older," she snickered. "But seriously, when were you born?"

"Nineteen-seventy-two. I'm forty-seven years old. You?"

Her lips pressed into a tight line. Should she tell him the truth? Why not? After all, he read the red leather book. "I was born in the year of our Lord, fourteen- hundred-fifty-six. I'm five-hundred-sixty-three years old."

She wasn't sure what the look on his face meant, was he shocked? Was he deciding whether or not she was teasing? "I win! I'm definitely older," she tried to make another joke.

"Damn, I like older women, but." He held his serious face for a fraction of a second longer before erupting into a boisterous, easy laughter that warmed Brigid from the inside out. "No, but seriously, how old are you?"

The Sacrifice

"I'm telling the truth and if what I suspect is correct, you'll finally believe me when you turn one hundred without aging another day."

He stopped gathering their clothes long enough to search her eyes. "Hmm, I'll have to take your word on that."

Den pulled on his jeans, grinning as he stared openly at her body. Without breaking their gaze, he knelt and used his handkerchief to wipe the clear, warm liquid he had filled her with as it was snaking its way down her inner thigh. He cleaned her with a loving intimacy that was strange for so new a romance; gently rubbing the tender skin, spreading her folds and wiping them clean, and then blowing softly to finish drying the trails of his desire. Brigid wondered if Den felt it, too; this immediate bond.

"Do you know what I just realized?" he asked, still kneeling at her feet. His hand slid up her calf muscle then back down to her ankle. "You said you love blue eyes. Yours is greenish-yellow. You know when you mix green and yellow it makes blue, right?"

She gave him a smug grin, slowly blinking her eyes as she savored the sight of him kneeling in front of her. "No, it doesn't."

"Yes, it does."

"No," Brigid laughed. "If you mix blue and yellow you get green."

He shrugged nonchalantly, preparing to

stand. "Either way, its evidence we were somehow fated. Instead of being written in the stars, its written in the color of our eyes."

Brigid's smile broadened. *So, he does feel it, too!*

For a moment, they just looked at each other. In any other situation, it would have been an awkward moment, but for some reason, Brigid was completely at ease with this splendid man regarding her like she was his most prized possession.

Suddenly, she saw his expression change, and her stomach lurched with fear. He looked over her shoulder at something behind her and started to stand.

"What the fuck…?"

Then all went black.

***

She was freezing. Was her neck broken? It felt useless, rubbery. She tried to force her eyes open, but her sight was blurred by thick tears. A sharp pain was shooting from between her shoulder blades to the base of her skull and there was a muffled noise pulling her from her unconscious state.

"Miss Whelan!"

"Miss Whelan, are you alright, ma'am?" She heard a man and a woman calling her name,

The Sacrifice

asking her questions. She tried to raise her head to look up, but the pain instantly stopped her.

"Easy now, ma'am, you're head's bleeding. Hold still while I get you out of these cuffs." It was the woman's voice this time.

Brigid was trying to make sense of what the voices were saying. Her head was bleeding? Where was Den? Why couldn't she feel her arms? Why was it so cold? She heard the clank of metal as the cuffs released and she fell face first in the damp leaves.

"Ma'am!" the woman screeched. "Oh my god, Jeffrey, help! Get her shoulder. Easy!" There was pressure in the back of her head as the woman pressed a cloth to a wound. A sharp pain made her suck air between her teeth. "I'm sorry, ma'am, but I have to stop this bleeding. Quite a knot you have here."

Jeffrey? Yes, Brigid knew that name. It was the caretakers; Jeffrey and Mindy Forde! She felt a rush of relief as her senses began returning.

"Ok, now, try to move your arms, Miss Whelan," Jeffrey spoke calmly, no doubt attempting to keep the two women from hysterics. "Can you move them at all?"

Brigid was now lying on her side, her head still in its bent position. She tried to move her right arm, her eyes squeezing shut to buffer against the agony of limbs deprived of blood supply. The stabbing pin pricks as tissues were hydrated with

Christy Lynn

precious fluids once again, was nearly unbearable. She held her breath and attempted to lift her head.

How long had she been bound to that tree? It had to have been hours. By the look of the violet sky it was late evening, shortly after sunset. Thank god she had texted the Fordes when she and Dennis first started on their walk that morning.

Mindy was rubbing her neck gently and assisted her in straightening it. Brigid could see there was more than just concern for her welfare in both the caretakers' eyes. "What is it?" she tried to speak, but her throat was so dry it came out as a croaking sound.

"Miss Whelan, did..." Jeffrey paused, looking up at the sky then back at her once again. His jaw was clamped shut; he seemed mad as hell. "Did that man you brought here do this to you? I'll kill him for you, ma'am, I swear it."

"He can do it, too. Jeffrey was a sniper in the Gulf War. Hell of a marksman. There'd be no evidence, not a trace, ma'am. No one would ever know," Mindy added.

"Wait. What?" Brigid sat up slowly, rubbing her forehead. She could feel something crusty on her face and picked it off. Dried blood. "Where is he?" she questioned, reaching for Mindy's hands for assistance to stand.

"I'm sorry, Miss Whelan, but he left. It looks as though he took your car, too. I don't know what

The Sacrifice

kind of man does something like this, but he's got an ass whipping coming." Jeffrey appeared on her left side and linked his arm under hers for support. Mindy was on her right. They made their way up the path toward the cabin.

Brigid shook her head slowly. It didn't make sense. Den wouldn't do this to her, would he? Truth be told, she didn't know him at all, but at the same time, she felt she knew him as intimately as if they'd been together forever. "No. something isn't right. Den wouldn't do this."

The Fordes helped her up the porch steps and into the cabin. Mindy rushed to get the first aid kit while Jeffrey sat Brigid on the couch. "At least, he had the decency to leave a note, ma'am." Mindy handed her a sealed envelope.

Anxiously, Brigid tore it open, her face turning pale as she read it. "Oh my god," she whispered.

Miss Whelan,

You should take better care than to steal my car. It has an after-market tracking system I personally installed. Thank you for keeping Mr. Markham safe, as I'm sure you're aware Miss Fainn has need of him.

Marshall Murphy

"Oh my god, they took him!" Brigid gasped.

Christy Lynn

"Please, I need your truck."

"Of course, ma'am. We'll take the quad-runner home. Get it back to us when you can." Mindy took her hand, patting it reassuringly.

Jeffrey bent to look Brigid in the eyes. "You probably have a concussion, ma'am. I don't think you should drive." His eyes darted back and forth as he assessed the size of her pupils. "Are you sure you're ok? The city is four hours away, ma'am."

"Please stop calling me ma'am!" she snapped. She didn't mean to be so snippy, but the frustration of being hours away from Den at a time like this was beginning to take hold. There was no telling what could have happened to him already. Even if the Fordes did let her borrow their truck, she'd never make it back to the Tower in time to save Dennis from becoming Lilith's sacrifice.

"Is there any other way I can get to him? Jeff, he's in serious danger. He didn't do this to me, he's been kidnapped and his life is in danger."

Jeffrey exchanged a look of indecision with his wife. With a heavy sigh, he ran his hand through his hair and rubbed the back of his neck. "Alright," he sighed. "I'll call a friend of mine who lives near here. He has a helicopter, runs these tourist trips through the mountains. If you're sure it's an emergency..."

"It is!" Brigid interrupted. She was so grateful, she wanted to kiss him. "The Tower has a heli-pad

The Sacrifice

on the roof. We'll be able to safely land. Let your friend know I'll pay any price for his help."

"While Jeffrey makes the necessary calls, let's get you cleaned up, ma'am," Mindy suggested. She went into the bathroom and a few minutes later Brigid heard the wisshh of water from the shower.

***

It was so much darker in the country than in the city; owed to the absence of electric light. The stars were so abundant here. Brigid let her head fall back so she could see the entirety of the night sky. Suddenly, she wished Den could see this; a whole galaxy of god knows what, stretching out as farther than the eye could see. Jeffrey Forde said his friend would meet them within the hour, and so they sat in a clearing - waiting - while Den was being prepared to give his life for the satisfaction of another.

Brigid shivered, even though it wasn't cold. Still staring at the stars above, she closed her eyes and saw the constellations etched on the dark canvases of her lids. An owl hooted from a stand of trees not far away; how long had it been since she'd heard such a beautiful, mournful sound; eighteen-hundred-thirty? Surely not! She had most assuredly heard an owl since then. But, for some reason, sitting on a porch in twilight on a

Christy Lynn

humid, summer evening in eighteen-hundred-thirty was the last time she could recall an encounter with such an omen as the night avian.

People back then were superstitious of night creatures, but not Brigid. Often times, such iconic symbols of doom and bad luck seemed to have the opposite effect in Brigid's life. She broke a mirror once and instead of seven years of bad luck, she found an enormous, gold nugget in a creek in the Oregon Territory that same day! She looked forward to black cats crossing her path because there has never been a time such an occurrence took place that she didn't end up meeting some dashing, virile man and having the pleasure of absorbing his chi shortly after the feline took its stroll.

The evening the owl landed on her porch railing was the first time the owl lived up to its ominous reputation for her.

She rubbed her arms to dispel the chill that had unexpectedly crept up on her and glanced around the lonely glade. The meadow was of good size, big enough for the helicopter to land without difficulty. It was completely surrounded by forest, and shrouded as it was in a deep purple haze, she could swear she'd been here before...some other time.

Brigid leaned against the tailgate of the Forde's Ford pick-up truck, tilting her head as if she could hear the jingling of harness rigging and

The Sacrifice

the creaking of a wooden carriage as it lumbered over one rut, just to fall into another immediately following the last. She recalled walking along a road in North Carolina, constantly keeping to the edges as it was a busy thoroughfare and the morning crowds were traveling into town to sell their wares and produce.

She was struggling most uncomfortably with a large basket full of apples; a gift from the wife of the reverend of the local parish. The reverend's parish home had a small orchard that the woman was most proud of, and she never missed an opportunity to share the bounty with fellow parishioners. Brigid was most definitely grateful for the fruit, but considering the walk home, rather wished the reverend's wife would have had her husband deliver the basket during one of his many uninvited visits.

However, had the lovely reverend's wife done so, Brigid would never have made the acquaintance of Mr. Mathis Bouchard, and would have missed out meeting one of her favorite of the men she encountered in her life. He appeared to her on the road like the proverbial white knight, poised to rescue any damsels in distress. She'd been limping along under the weight of the basket, shoulders up to her ears from the strain, when a huge, black horse trotted right up to her - as it was guided to do by its rider, of course – and stuck its long nose in the pile of apples! She watched in shock as the animal sank its long, yellowed teeth into the first one it encountered and plucked it neatly from the basket, drool slinging over the hard fruit and dripping onto the dust of the road as it chewed.

"My apologies, Madame," Mr. Bouchard grunted as he dismounted the large beast. "He's a terrible thief." With reigns in hand, he began to walk beside Brigid - uninvited. She tried to ignore the nuisance of yet another man attempting to 'make her acquaintance' since she and Barrex had arrived in the Appalachian settlement.

Single women in need of a husband were scarce, especially indescribably beautiful ones. So, Barrex found himself most popular among the male population...everyone wanted to be his friend. He tired quickly of men constantly hinting at wanting an invitation to dinner. It was a wonderful source of entertainment for both Brigid and Barrex to watch a new acquaintance pretend to be surprised that Barrex had a sister living with him and that she was not the reason they wished to attend dinner in the first place.

Brigid wanted to pretend she was her brother's lover, you know, to stir up gossip and intrigue, but Barrex vehemently denied her the pleasure of such a charade. He was too worried it would ruin his reputation and cripple his chances of getting laid. No doubt, he'd been right to insist she not entertain such notions; bigotry was severely frowned upon among the Quakers and exiled, alike, and came with severe punishment.

"My name is Mathis Bouchard, I'm most pleased to..."

"Here," Brigid cut him off and plucked another fat apple from the basket, handing it to Mr. Bouchard. "He's a big enough creature, he'll want another before long." She nodded her head at the horse.

Mr. Bouchard smiled, tipping his hat kindly. "Thank you, madam. Might I tell Brutus the name of his thoughtful benefactress?"

Brigid gave him a look, a small smile touching her lips. Perhaps Mr. Bouchard wasn't as dull as the others. He seemed clever enough not to allow her to end the conversation before it even began, as she was trying to do. "His name is Brutus, eh?" she craned her neck to look around Mr. Bouchard at the horse's face. "Listen here, Brutus, there is not a thing to be done for the apple you rudely stole right under my nose, but I am warning you to think twice before attempting to duplicate such a theft. I'm rather fond of horse meat."

Mr. Bouchard erupted in a most engaging laugh. It had such a carefree, easy sound to it that Brigid was unable to resist joining him, covering her mouth prettily with her gloved hand as she giggled. "My name is Brigid Whelan. Pleased to make your acquaintance, Mr. Bouchard."

She paused walking long enough to offer her

Christy Lynn

hand in greeting. Mr. Bouchard bent low to kiss her knuckle, as was proper, and when he rose to look at her, she saw he possessed a most stunning shade of blue eyes. He caught her gaping at him, which made her blush sweetly.

"My word, Miss Whelan, but you are an angel from Heaven above," Mr. Bouchard breathed. That was all it took, he was immediately, desperately in love.

After only two weeks, Mathis Bouchard asked Brigid to be his wife. She happily accepted his proposal. Mathis possessed a wonderful sense of humor, and was not so stuffy as many of the colonists she'd met along her travels. He had a love of life that Brigid found refreshing, and through the weeks of knowing him, was able to renew her own love of the world around her. She felt good in his presence, healthy. It was as if she had been a starving beggar in a gutter and a kind soul from a mission appeared to give her food and drink.

Mathis was a kind man who owned a winery back home in France, which meant he could provide a comfortable life for them both. They never married, unfortunately. Mathis was attacked and robbed on the same road where they shared their first encounter. The bastards who set upon him, shot him over a gold pocket watch and a few insignificant coins not amounting to much. Mathis was found dead in a ditch, his horse

The Sacrifice

standing over him as if waiting for him to get up and lead him onward. Mathis was still clutching a bouquet of wildflowers...he was unfailing in gifting her with flowers every single time he came to see her.

Brigid had been sitting on the porch waiting for him to arrive for dinner; an invitation Mathis never missed. The sun had just dipped behind the western ridgeline when an owl sailed quietly from the sky above and set itself gently on the porch railing. It hooted twice before taking flight once again, the eerie sound made her scalp tingle. As soon as the bird disappeared into the night woods, the sound of hooves bringing the news of death reached her.

Christy Lynn

CHAPTER 13

Brigid's mind wandered to the words of wisdom her mother had written for her and Barrex in the red, leather book. She had been wondering if she would ever find true love, and if she did, could she bear it? She'd never had such a concern before, but now, she began to entertain the thought of an eternal bond with a man who shared her plight.

Succubi and incubi cannot bear children the same way humans do. An incubus does not normally ejaculate when having an orgasm, therefore, he needs the competing sperm of a human male to draw his sperm out. So, when a succubus finds a man she thinks would be a suitable sperm donor, she has sex with him, retains his seed in the warmth of her innermost folds and then takes it to her incubus mate. At which time, he would coat his member with the mortal seed and have sex with a human woman in hopes his own sperm does its job and impregnates her. The couple then keeps a close eye on the pregnant woman until she gives birth. Traditionally, the succubus would drain the birth mother to death after she delivers and claim the infant as her own.

Brigid thought of her mother; a simple human

The Sacrifice

susceptible to the charms of an incubus. How tormenting to endure watching her husband - the love of her life - have sex with other women to stay healthy and alive. She wasn't sure if she could bear seeing Den holding another. Would their bond be strong enough that it wouldn't matter? Could she rationalize that it was only a necessity, and not for pleasure? Would Den be able to share her, in return?

Suddenly, Brigid realized something; Den washed her inner thighs clean of his sperm! She knows he's an incubus, can feel it in her soul, so how was it he emitted semen during an orgasm? He was such a mystery to her, but one she was happy to spend eternity solving.

She swallowed hard, letting the pinpoints of light in the night sky blur as she relaxed her eyes. Silently, she prayed to Lilith; please, dear Goddess, don't take him. I'm a faithful follower of your grace, as you are the creator of all succubi. Reward me with this favor? I have never asked anything of you, or your power. I ask you this...refrain from the sacrifice and give Dennis Markham to me.

The tip of her nose burned as tears gathered on her lashes. Mindy nudged her, offering a bottle of water, which she gratefully accepted, sniffling to keep her nose from running. She took a long drink, nearly choking when her cell phone vibrated in her back pocket, catching her by

Christy Lynn

surprise.

"Barry, oh my god, they found us and took Den!" There was no stopping the tears once she saw her brother's number on the screen.

"I know." He sounded strange. "Look, Blue, as long as you stay away from the Tower and the celebration tonight, nothing will happen to me."

Her face contorted in anger. "Nothing will happen to you?" she questioned. Then she understood. "Where are they keeping you?"

"He's fine, Brigid. He's with me." Anne's familiar voice answered her question from the other end of the line. "I love you and Barrex as if you were my own flesh and blood and I wish no harm for either of you. So, listen closely; for your own good, extend your vacation in the mountains."

"Anne," Brigid's voice trembled with anger. "Let Barrex go. I'm not asking, I'm telling. I'll be outside the front entrance of the Tower in a couple of hours and as long as Barrex is waiting by the fountain for me," she paused a moment before finishing her sentence. "That'll be the end of it."

She heard Anne's sharp laugh. "Is that so? You're telling me you'll just walk away, even though I have your toy?"

There was a moment of silence as Brigid thought carefully what to say. She was winging it, having no idea what to do. "Well...I'd like to attend the celebration."

The Sacrifice

"Hell no," Anne immediately replied.

"Look, bitch, I'm not about to face one hundred years of Lilith's wrath! There's no way I'm going to risk offending her. The whole coven will be there, I'm a little outnumbered, wouldn't you agree? So what can I possibly do? As a creation of Lilith, herself, I'm required to be there."

It was Anne's turn to be silent. Brigid bit her lip, desperately hoping Anne would agree. No matter how the night was to end, she wanted to see this through with Den. She had to be near him. "And you want me to believe you'll just stand by and watch as your piece of ass is sacrificed?"

"About that..." Brigid tentatively spoke. "Are you sure you should go through with your plan to offer him up? He's been tainted by another succubus's touch; I fucked him for hours...several times. You know the rules."

"As far as the Goddess is concerned, what she doesn't know won't hurt her. He is hers, Brigid Whelan, not yours. I'm going to receive her blessings like never before for this and your crush isn't going to ruin it."

Brigid quietly consented, "Fine."

"Tell me you swear upon your honor to participate and not intervene."

How would she be able to do this? She came from a time when a person's honor meant everything; it meant everything to her, always

Christy Lynn

has. But she realized, quite suddenly, that Dennis Markham meant more than her honor...more than her life.

"I swear upon my honor," she spat. Quickly, she hung up before anymore could be said. At the moment, she had made it clear she was coming to the Tower and she didn't want Anne to have time to change her mind.

***

The city was gorgeous from the perspective of the helicopter hovering high above in preparation to land on the roof of the Tower, but Brigid couldn't appreciate the twinkling display of electric beauty. She was leaning forward in her seat, hand already resting on the door latch.

"Miss Whelan, we're here, just relax. You'll be on your way in a moment," Jeffrey seized her wrist and removed it from the safety handle, no doubt worried she would prematurely pop the door and get them all killed.

The helicopter shook as it came to rest on the helipad. Brigid tore off the headphones and was on her feet before Jeffrey even unbuckled his safety belt. As soon as the pilot opened the door, she jumped out, accidentally bumping her head on the way. "Fuck! Damn that hurts!" She rubbed the knot on her head that had risen about an inch above her scalp. Whoever was responsible for giving it to her would pay.

The pilot stared at her with a disapproving look. "What? Never heard a woman cuss before?" Brigid yelled at him above the roar of the swirling blades. "Well, fuck your snooty ass!"

Jeffrey laughed out loud and slapped his friend on the shoulder. He made some hand signal to him, asking him to wait a moment, then quickly escorted Brigid safely away from the danger of decapitation. There were two doors leading from the roof; one was to an elevator that had access to all the floors and was for the express use of the coven. The other led to an elevator that accessed the lobby, requiring a visitor to check in with security before proceeding. Brigid swiped her pass key, nothing. She did it again, the light on the lock panel flashed red, denying her entry into the coven elevator.

"Fine, I see how it is now. Well, main elevator, it is," she huffed, nearly punching the "down" button that would take her to the lobby.

Jeffrey stood by quietly and when the doors opened, prepared to step inside. "Thank you, Jeff, but you go on home," Brigid stepped in ahead of him, pushing the button marked L for lobby.

"Are you sure, ma'am? I think you may need my help." He looked concerned, not ready to leave her unattended.

The doors were closing as she waved him off. "I'm fine. Thank you and Mindy for everything!"

Christy Lynn

she said, before they closed tightly, dividing her from her worried, ex-military groundskeeper.

Marshall Murphy was waiting in the massive lobby, hands clasped in front of him and looking extra fine in a black suit. Brigid stepped out of the elevator and gave him a look. "Nice to see you again, Miss Whelan," he smiled.

"Cut the crap, Marshall," she snapped.

"Did you like the way my car handled?" he asked, a note of sarcasm in his tone. "Hugs the road, doesn't it?"

"I'm warning you, don't."

Mr. Murphy, Head of Security for the Tower, was a force to be reckoned with, but he was also wise. When a succubus threatens your well being, you listen. So, he wisely shut his mouth and stood there patiently watching her.

"Well, where is everyone? Where am I supposed to go?" Brigid could hardly stand still.

"The celebration is in the main ballroom. This way," Mr. Murphy offered to escort her.

"I know where the ballroom is. I designed it, for god's sake." Brigid stormed past him, stomping through the vacant lobby, the thick, rubber soles of her hiking boots squeaking loudly on the marble flooring. "Shit!"

"Anything wrong, Miss?" Marshall asked, nearly trotting to keep up with her determined strides.

"Look at my outfit. I'm not

dressed...whatever, it doesn't matter." Her gaze swept the length of her body and she rolled her eyes. With her affinity to fashion, it bothered her to show up at a black tie event in jeans and sweatshirt.

Brigid pushed the double doors to the massive ballroom open wide, drawing the attention of everyone nearby. She was aware of the looks she was getting, but ignored them. She was here for Dennis and Barrex, no one else mattered. Anxious, she stood on her toes, trying to see over heads taller than hers. Barrex and Anne were nowhere to be found.

Mad as a hornet, Brigid whirled to face Mr. Murphy, who was still clinging to her like static. "What the hell, Marshall? Stop wasting my time with this shit."

"You have quite a mouth when you're angry, Miss Whelan. You told Miss Fainn you wanted to attend the celebration," Marshall Murphy noted, waving his hand at the crowd. But seeing he had pressed his luck too far, quickly added, "Your brother and the others are in the penthouse."

"Then why am I down here?" she screeched.

Everyone stopped to stare. There were hundreds of people she didn't know, dressed in their finest and enjoying what they believed to be just another great, Manhattan party. Members of the coven were mingling with their invited, human guests, brushing against them or taking

Christy Lynn

them to private corners to partake in a little more than casual contact could provide.

Mr. Murphy clenched his jaw and grabbed her upper arm, ushering her briskly from the ballroom before the scene escalated. He pulled her into the hall, his face red with anger and embarrassment. "What in god's name has gotten into you?" he hissed, giving her a shake. "I've never seen you behave in such a way!"

"That's because you've never seen our dear Brigid in love before, Marshall."

Brigid yanked her arm free from Marshall's grasp and turned to face Anne. "Where is he?"

"No concern for your brother?" Anne chided. "Hundreds of years by your side and you forget him as soon as a great lay rattles your teeth? How ungrateful."

"It was my brother I was referring to."

"No, it wasn't." Anne snickered.

Brigid's nostrils flared but she wisely held her tongue, knowing she was too mad to be rational, and saying the wrong thing could get her escorted right out of the building. She fought to control her temper, meeting Anne's gaze with a cool look of self control. "Barry can take care of himself," she said softly.

"Is that so?" Anne poked at Brigid's fragile facade. "Come with me, your brother would like to see you."

"Where's Den?" Brigid asked, stepping into

The Sacrifice

the private elevator leading to the penthouse. She received no answer to her query.

They rode several floors upward in silence, Anne standing in the center, Mr. Murphy to her right, and Brigid shaking with nervous fury on the left. Anne turned to her security guard, seemingly ignoring Brigid's presence altogether. She stepped close to him, looking up at the once gorgeous man.

"Baby," she whispered, resting a hand on his chest. He stared down at her intently as Brigid watched with incredulous anger; what did Anne think she was doing? But the anger turned to immediate concern for Marshall's welfare. Brigid knew what Anne was capable of and she had the habit of trying to shock Brigid whenever the opportunity presented itself. Regardless of Mr. Murphy doing what was necessary to keep his job, she was very fond of him and didn't wish him harm.

"You know what elevators do to me," Anne teased him.

The very corner of Marshall's mouth turned upward in a small grin. "Yes, Mistress, I do."

Mistress. The word sent chills down Brigid's spine. For the first time in her life, she hated the sound of it. Anne suddenly reached a hand to the control panel and hit the emergency stop button.

"Hey!" Brigid started to protest, but fell silent. Neither Anne, nor Marshall Murphy, were paying any attention to her, whatsoever.

"You know what to do," Anne smiled coyly.

Marshall Murphy looked suddenly uneasy, glancing in Brigid's direction. "Mistress?" he questioned, making a subtle nod in their guest's direction.

Anne glanced over her shoulder at Brigid pressed in the corner, trying to get as far away from them as possible. "I see," she breathed.

She smashed herself against the tall man's body, backing him against the wall. Brigid watched as Anne compelled Marshall the same way she did Den that night in the club. She took his hand in hers and placed her other hand on the back of his neck. He bent his head and kissed her.

Brigid backed into the corner and slid to the floor. Whatever game Anne was playing, she was unmercifully her pawn, as were they all; nothing to do but wait. Frustrated, she wrapped her arms around her drawn knees and put her forehead against them, not wanting to witness what was about to take place.

Now fully compelled, Marshall Murphy lost the reserve necessary of a security agent. Anne had successfully aroused him, her hand rubbing the bulge in his pants while consuming his tongue. He wrapped his strong arms around Anne's waist, crushing her against him. Her sudden moans piqued Brigid's curiosity and, against her will, she peeked. She inhaled sharply,

The Sacrifice

feeling the stir of arousal.

Marshall was clenching fistfuls of Anne's long gown, his mouth devouring her neck as her head bent to the side to receive it. Anne pushed away, sitting down hard on the tiny, red chaise along the back wall. Brigid suddenly understood why it was there in the first place. She'd always thought it was stupid to put furniture in an elevator as small as this one. If a person couldn't stand for the amount of time it took to get from the lobby to a floor above, then they needed to be in a nursing home, not a condo! Now she knew its purpose.

A wicked smile spread across Anne's face as her legs spread for Marshall Murphy. Her lovely, red gown stretched against her knees, modestly concealing what Brigid had no desire to see from her perspective on the floor.

Marshall stripped off his suit coat and knelt in front of Anne, pushing the ball gown to her tiny waist. The Head Mistress leaned back, closing her eyes and draping her long legs over Marshall's shoulders. Without foreplay or preamble, he slipped her panties to the side and leaned in.

Brigid watched the muscles of his back working beneath his white, button-down dress shirt. He was wearing a black shoulder holster that boasted a Sig Sauer .45 caliber. She found gun holsters over dress shirts particularly sexy, having a clothing fetish. Powerful men were another fetish, considering no matter how powerful they were, she could easily kill them. The fetish of such men coming in the disguise of hope...hope for one day to find a man who was her match; her search was finally over - Dennis Markham.

She found Anne's shapely calves draped over Marshall's shoulders begrudgingly erotic. Marshall was always attractive to her, until recently; the effects of being slowly drained of his chi unfortunately taking its toll. If she wasn't harboring such venomous hatred toward Anne, at the moment, she might have been able to have found pleasure in the scene unfolding before her.

"Ohh, my god, he's so good at this, Brigid. Want to try him?" Anne goaded Brigid, watching her with that wicked expression. Brigid raised her chin, meeting Anne's gaze defiantly and sneered. Anne's eyes rolled upward and her lids squeezed shut. She buried her fingers in Marshall's hair, moving her hips to the rhythm of his tongue.

Brigid quickly looked away.

"Faster, baby...short on time tonight," Anne panted.

Brigid buried her face in her forearms, the sounds of sucking and licking too loud and discernable in the eight-foot by eight-foot confines of the still elevator. Against her will, her clitoris began to throb. She wanted to yank Marshall from between Anne's legs and shove his face between her own; but Den's face was most

The Sacrifice

prevalent in her mind. No matter how tempting a simple act of nothing more than physical pleasure might be, she really didn't want anyone - or anything - except him.

Anne's whimpers turned into coaching cries as she urged Marshall onward. "Yes! Baby, yes! So good! Right there," she whined.

Brigid let one eye open just enough to peek. She saw Anne's perfect up do falling in loose tendrils around her face, where a becoming sheen of thin perspiration misted her forehead. Her eyes were squeezed shut, fists gripping handfuls of Marshall's short, dark hair.

Brigid's panties were becoming uncomfortably wet. She was a succubus, spurred by nature to engage in sex; she needed it! But she needed Den more, and fought against the hunger building deep inside.

"Are you done yet?" she snapped, letting her head fall back against the wall.

Neither heard a word she said. Anne was so close to her climax; the signs being easily read. She was rubbing her vagina on Marshall's entire face, which seemed to heighten his own excitement even more. He suddenly unzipped his pants and Brigid saw him reach around his waist, his elbow beginning to move up and down, stroking himself in that telltale motion.

Anne was oblivious, her whimpers now full-on cries of ecstasy. Suddenly, her whole body

Christy Lynn

spasmed and she erupted. "Now, baby, now!" she rasped.

Marshall quickly straightened his back and thrust his cock inside her. It took only a few pumps to bring him to his climax, but Brigid admired the way he handled Anne. He grabbed her roughly by the back of the neck, shoved his cock deep inside her, and held her firmly in place as he briskly pounded. Brigid heard a soft, quick growl escape the man's throat and it was over.

Slowly, she got to her feet, folding her arms across her chest and turning her back on the pair as they composed themselves. "I'm sorry you had to see that," Marshall mumbled, as he tucked his shirt into his trousers.

Brigid shrugged nonchalantly. "You'd be surprised how often I've seen Anne fuck a face." She hated that her remark might hurt him. She didn't like to be mean, but she hoped he didn't think he was Annaline Fainn's only toy.

"Remember Bernard?" Anne suddenly laughed. "Or shall I say Saint Bernard!"

Brigid was glad her back was still to Anne, because she didn't want her to see the smile that couldn't be stopped. Bernard Sampson was a lover from Anne's past; during a time when Anne and Brigid were good friends. The women nicknamed him Saint Bernard because of his name, his fluffy size, and his oral sex technique; Anne joked it was like being licked by a dog!

The Sacrifice

Knowing Anne was the key to safely returning Barrex and Den, Brigid seized the opportunity to perhaps get on her good side. Threatening the Head Mistress and trying to force her to give her what she wanted wasn't getting her anywhere, so she decided to try a different strategy. Considering Anne had just had an orgasm, perhaps she would be in a more generous mood.

"Woof," Brigid softly barked.

Anne burst into laughter. "Oh my god, I can't believe you remember that!" To further their secret jest, they would bark quietly whenever Bernard was around.

After centuries of living, one has to be creative in order to amuse oneself. Brigid and Anne began nicknaming every man they managed to keep around longer than a night. It became quite a game, even Barrex joined in eventually. He still nicknames his conquests...such as Freak; the man he caught stealing in his apartment only days prior.

"The only St. Bernard in history to own a Cocker Spaniel," Brigid snickered.

"That's right! I loved that little dog, such a sweetie," Anne replied, still laughing.

"Ya know, there's still good times to be had," Marshall chimed in, unable to resist the opportunity to perhaps bring the once close friends back together again. Brigid cut her eyes over her shoulder at him - if only he knew.

Christy Lynn

PART TWO

The Sacrifice

CHAPTER 14

The Abbot of Glenstal Abbey in County Limerick was a most fearsome-looking man. Upon seeing him enter the house, Brigid slipped out the back door and hid behind the pigpen. She was resolved to take her packed belongings and journey abroad, even if Barrex would not accompany her. There was no way she was going with a man who claimed to be a servant of the Anglo-Saxon God, but possessed the eyes of a demon!

Her mother had written a letter nearly two weeks prior to Abbot Eoghan Doyle, begging him to harbor Brigid and Barrex in the safe confines of Glenstal Abbey. The villagers had become suspicious of her little family and the accusations of witchcraft stirred the mobs. As the weeks passed, suspicion manifested into action.

At the tender age of sixteen, Brigid was experiencing her sexual awakening. Boys were no longer a nuisance, tugging her braids or stealing the little pies she baked and sat on the window sill to cool. They had become noticeable; catching her eye when they came to hunt or visit with Barrex.

One young man in particular, Colin McCarthy, happened to notice Brigid, in return. He was a brawny lad with dark hair and eyes as sharp and

The Sacrifice

blue as the Irish sky. For an entire week he showed up every morning, leaning against the door frame of the Whelan cottage, staring at Brigid while Barrex finished his breakfast and hurried to collect his bow and arrows.

Of course, their mother was aware of the sheepish glances her daughter was casting at young Colin...and the wolfish stares the boy was giving her daughter in return. Brigid would pretend to be most intent upon washing the dishes and clearing the table, all the while, constantly sneaking a peek at the hulk of a boy filling the space of the entryway.

Finally, one evening when the boys returned with a bounty of rabbits tied to a pole between them, Colin found the opportunity he had patiently been waiting for; a moment alone with Brigid. Barrex tossed his end of the pole to the ground and ran off to the outhouse in a state of renal emergency, leaving Colin in the yard to tend to their kills.

Colin started untying the little carcasses in preparation to skin the hides, just as Brigid emerged from their little house nestled in the deep forest. The sun was still at least an hour from setting, but shrouded by trees as the Whelan cottage was, the light was quickly fading, sheathing them in an intimate, gray haze.

She was carrying a bowl of hazelnuts, already cracked and pried from their shells. "Hungry at all?" she asked, much too quietly. Her voice was beginning to adopt the sultry quality of a full-grown woman.

Colin, holding a rabbit by the neck in one hand and knife in the other, looked up at her and quickly severed the rope that attached the carcass to the pole. "Famished," he said, giving her a grin that suggested he was not referring to his stomach.

"I gathered these m'self for yer return. It might hold ye until supper, if ye care to join us?" she asked, keeping her eyes cast to the ground so her long, dark lashes rested on her cheeks in a flirtatious way.

Colin stood, towering above her; he was very tall for his age. She felt a shiver wash over her from his sudden closeness and found she couldn't look him in the eyes...those beautiful, blue eyes. An intense feeling of elation spread through her chest at the thought of maybe one day sharing a life with this young man. He was so big and strong; all the girls in the village would hate her on her wedding day! She'd heard tell of several of the village's young ladies were already engaged. Brigid wondered if they were in love with their betrothed, as she was with Colin?

Shyly, she offered the bowl.

Colin reached for it, his fingers intentionally covering hers. He paused, not taking the bowl from her, but just looking at her as they touched.

The Sacrifice

his large fingers moved slowly over the tips of hers, caressing her knuckles, nails, and skin. The heat rose in her cheeks, confirming his inkling that she did, in fact, like him.

The outhouse door slammed shut as Barrex emerged, looking relieved. He tossed up a hand and waved at his sister. "Meet me on the road at sunset," Colin quickly whispered, before Barrex could crush his chance to make such a private liaison.

Brigid gave him a slight nod, undetected by her brother as he sauntered up, giving the two of them a questionable look. "Boil these for our supper, Blue," he smiled, proud of their bounty.

He handed her two large rabbits, which she refused to take. "I am not skinning those. Bring them to me when they are properly prepared," she snipped, turning to head to the house and tossing her hair over her shoulders as she did so.

The boys chuckled and set to work on the kills. "She's a spirited lass, yer sister," Colin remarked, avoiding Barrex's sudden, suspicious glare.

"Yes...she is," he answered slowly. "But no more spirited than yer own sisters."

"True enough," Colin agreed, trying to seem innocent in his observation.

Colin left shortly after supper, and Brigid made some excuse about wanting to return to the hazelnut tree she'd discovered earlier that day, before it got too dark. Since the boys had eaten her first harvest, she needed to gather more so in order to make a loaf for tomorrow. She hurried down the path through the dense forest that led to the main thoroughfare of the village. Most of the locals lived in the village or took up tenancies on the rolling farm lands to the west. But not the Whelan's, their mother preferred the seclusion of the deep woods to the ever-watching eyes of the parishioners.

Obviously, their preference of homesteads rose the concern and suspicion of the God-fearing; no one pure of heart would chose to live in the dark forests where faeries and demons dwelled. Yet, the Whelan's seemed to reside unharmed and in peace...much to the villagers' dismay.

Brigid rushed along the side of the road, eyes sweeping from side to side in pursuit of Colin McCarthy. He suddenly jumped out from behind a large tree and grabbed her around the waist to drag her back behind the large oak with him. She had no idea what to expect, having no knowledge of intimacy, but eager, willing, and consumed by her first love, she allowed Colin to push her against the wide tree trunk and kiss her.

Something ignited inside her, a passion that bloomed and combusted into a bonfire as her hormones surged from his touch. She was yet a maiden with dreams of true love and a small cottage filled with children. Anxiously, she

The Sacrifice

pushed at his chest, feeling there were things that should be said between them before sealing their love with affections such as these.

"I've been dreaming of ye, Colin," she whispered, smiling sweetly.

"Ye have?" Colin smiled broadly, his gaze glued to her bodice, instead of her eyes. "Oh, I've been dreaming of ye, too, lass."

He leaned in for another kiss, his assuming hands already poised to caress her bosom. "Do ye love me, Colin McCarthy?" Brigid asked, her tone insistent. This was a matter of great importance; a woman of virtue could only give herself to her husband, or one proposing such commitment. Brigid wanted the confirmation of Colin's intentions before proceeding.

His smile waned slightly but managed to hold. Quickly, he nodded in response and silenced her with his lips. His hands found the hem of her dress and it spiraled out of control from there. Brigid was consumed! She clung to the young man's strong body, wrapping herself around his torso and burying her hands in his tousled hair.

Her skirt was hiked up around her waist and Colin's heated palms were planted firmly on her buttocks. Suddenly, while she was rubbing herself against him, Colin managed to stick his cock inside her virgin pussy, breaking that most important piece of skin that determines an unwed woman's value. She gasped against the pain and

Christy Lynn

raked her nails across his shoulders, drawing blood as her succubus nature rushed to finally reveal itself.

Brigid's mouth sought Colin's, sucking his tongue as he thrust upward inside her. The poor lad had no idea what he had done - unleashing the curse of Lilith in a newly born succubus. His life would be payment for such a deed.

Colin was panting in her ear, grunting with each stroke. Even though Brigid was naive, she could feel something was about to happen. He was close to whatever it was he was thrusting inside her for. "I love ye, Colin McCarthy!" she breathed. "Say ye love me, too."

"I love ye, lass!"

"Tell me ye'll marry me! Say ye'll love me forever!" Her innocent heart was bursting with happiness.

"I- I'll make ye my wife if ye do this whenever I want," he panted. "Will ye let me inside ye whenever I wish it, woman? Were ye raised to please yer man? I'll teach ye how to kiss my cock!" he prattled on carelessly as his climax mounted. "I want ye again tomorrow, Brigid Whelan. Tell me ye'll let me inside ye tomorrow!"

Brigid was so lost in the moment, so filled with the young man, all she could do was seal her mouth around his, staring into those glittering, blue eyes as he moved inside her. The longer she kissed him, the stronger a feeling of euphoria built

The Sacrifice

in the very core of her being. So much so that she didn't realize Colin was weakening until she finally noticed the shine of his eyes dulling into a blank stare. Then, he fell to his knees, bringing her with him.

Together they collapsed into the thick fern carpet of the dark forest floor and Brigid rolled off of him, terrified for his well-being. Immediately, the thought they were being punished by the Gods for fornicating sprang to mind.

"Colin!" she cried. "We shall be doomed to dwell among the Mourning Fields of Hades for our wickedness!" Anxiously she searched his face, waiting for his reassurance and consolation that she was not to be a ruined woman by his hand.

When he did not respond, but lay limp, moaning as his eyes rolled about, she realized he was in peril. "Whatever is wrong w'ye, man?" She helped him to his feet, propping him against the tree trunk.

Immediately, she began a sort of triage, as she'd seen her mother do from time to time when the women from the village came to her for certain ailments and potions. She pressed her ear to his chest to listen to the beating of his heart.

"Y-ye are a witch! The devil's spawn!" Colin sputtered, gasping for the air to shout his accusations.

Brigid's eyes were wide with horror; what was happening to her love? The virile, young man's

Christy Lynn

body had suddenly withered! "No! No, do not dare say such a thing! Colin, it is I, Brigid Whelan, Barrex's sister. I am no witch."

"I-I..." he reached for his breeches but failed to grasp them in his weak hands. "I must warn the others."

He turned to the oak tree for help, using the rough bark to secure a finger hold and clamber to his feet. Brigid was horrified at his state of mind. He was so badly diminished he was staggering, but at this point, still possessing enough strength that he may have lived. He would have made it home to his village after a period of respite to regain the vitality that Brigid had unknowingly stolen.

But Brigid panicked.

What if what Colin said was true? Was there something evil about her? The Father of their parish preached against carnal pleasures, warning the younger generations that to even touch oneself was a sin, and she had been masturbating for several years as dreams of boys touching her body aided in her gratification.

Images of torches and spears in the night flashed through her mind; mobs on a witch hunt. She stood on the road, helpless, as Colin stumbled and fell, climbed to his feet, stumbled and fell again in his desperation to get to the village. "Ye cannot, Colin! Please! I've done not a thing wrong!" she shouted after him.

The Sacrifice

Suddenly, her temper flared and the words accusations he'd thrown at her sliced painful, hot wounds across her heart. Brigid marched up to him as he was again struggling to his feet. Her fists were planted firmly on her hips and she glared down at him in the dusty road. "Ye think ye can take my maidenhead, use me and leave me marked as a worthless whore?" she screamed. "Ye took the pleasure ye wanted, promised to marry me, and now think ye can escape the punishment of ruining me by making up such lies!"

Colin looked up at her, fear plain in his eyes. It was the first time she would witness such a look - the first of thousands. There he was, lying in the dusty road, naked from the waist down. His cock was done and so was he. He managed the strength to raise his fingers in the sign of the cross; warding off evil.

Brigid had no idea what made her do it, not knowing it was her natural instinct guiding her now...the same instinct that would see her through eons to come...but she sprang on the young man, straddling him and covering his mouth with hers. Colin may be finished with her, but she wasn't finished with him. The awakening was not yet complete.

She began rubbing her swollen clitoris along his fat, limp cock. She rode it, her eyes closing from the delicious feeling. The tingling began to build and against his will, she brought his

Christy Lynn

member back to life. Her slit, being adequately wet from his seed and her own arousal, caused no resistance when she shifted and slid him inside her needy depths.

The miraculous ability sex has to calm an angered soul and bring optimism where there is no hope, worked its magic on Brigid. She covered his face with her breasts and wrapped her arms around his head in a loving embrace. "We can be happy, Colin. I'll still be yer wife and we shall be together forever!" she panted, ignorantly thinking in her orgasmic state that she could make him forget. "Promise ye'll come to me tomorrow. Meet me here and we shall seal our bond as we make love again!"

But, as his face was buried in her bosom, she heard his muffled cries to the Heavens for help, and her dream of happiness with a loving husband and children vanished. "Damn ye to hell, Colin McCarthy," she whispered.

She leaned back to take one last look at him and saw the terror in his eyes. "What are ye?" he gasped.

Her jaw clenched tightly and her eyes narrowed. She slapped him hard across the face, then grabbed the collar of his shirt in both her fists. Heartbroken, and wanting one last kiss goodbye from her only true love, she covered his mouth with hers. As the remains of his life force rushed into her veins, her broken heart was

The Sacrifice

healed by the unyielding scar tissue of a love betrayed. The fire of a succubus's wrath sprang to life, consuming her as if she were a log of hickory, and she bit his lips until they bled. As she climbed off of his drained corpse, she spit the blood back on his face.

As she stood there, staring down at the waste of a body, her rage subsided. She was at odds with her emotions, being so violent only moments earlier, and now feeling sated from the act of physical pleasure. She began trembling from the realization of what had occurred. Her virginal blood smeared her inner thighs, running down her legs and leaving trails to her ankles. The tickling of it snagged her attention and upon seeing it, she sank to her knees on the road next to her dead lover, her breath suspended in agony.

She was ruined!

"Blue!"

Brigid heard Barrex yell her name in the darkness of the evening woods, but kept her forehead buried in the thick discs of dirt tilled by horses' hooves from previous travelers. She couldn't look up, not yet. She couldn't face what had just taken place. She was a murderess, an adulterer, and something vile. How could she ever look her brother and mother in the face again?

"Blue, speak to me, are ye alright?" Barrex dropped to the road beside his sister and shook her. "Colin!" he called out once, but seeing the

Christy Lynn

lifeless, blue stare of his friend's eyes, instantly knew it was futile to speak his name a second time.

With Barrex's help, Brigid sat up, her face sullied with dirt and the blood from Collin's lips smeared along her chin. "Barry, what is it? How did this happen?" her green, innocent eyes had taken on a yellowish cast that gave them a sinister, feline appearance. She was a fearsome sight to behold. "He said he loved me, Barry," she sobbed. "He said he'd make me his wife."

Barrex held her tighter. "Did he...did he have his way with ye?" he cautiously asked. Brigid didn't answer, which told him all he needed to know. "He deserves his fate, Blue. Don't ye waste precious tears on such a pig."

Without further discussion, he grabbed Colin's feet and dragged his heavy body into the dense, forest foliage. He left it lying in a thicket of ferns, adequately hidden from view of the road. He returned and grabbed his twin sister's hand, pulling her with him at a dead run back to the house - back to Mother.

Brigid learned that night what Barrex had already discovered months prior. As her mother wiped the telltale signs from Brigid's legs and face, she explained to her daughter the nature of her true heritage. She told her how she had prayed and hoped - against all hope - that her children would not be cursed from the seeds of their father,

The Sacrifice

but now that it was evident they were, much was to be said.

Barrex hadn't told his mother of the whore in Dublin he had accidentally drained five months ago, when he ran off with his friends to celebrate his sixteenth birthday. Normally, he celebrated with his sister, as they shared the same birthday, but becoming a man of sixteen, he felt the need to commemorate the passage in a different manner.

There had been two other lasses he had tried to have sex with, but saw the signs of their lives slipping away beneath the power of his kiss. He was able to stop his advances and leave each one unmolested and alive. Both girls were thoroughly stricken afterward, thinking it was the love they had for Barrex Whelan that made them swoon, not the compulsion of an Incubus.

An unfortunate fight ensued between both families of the girls, each claiming the right to boast that their daughter was soon to be engaged to the boy that dared take such liberties with her. The rift it caused in the parish is yet to be healed and will remain as such until Barrex makes his choice.

Mother knew though, even without Barrex confessing. She had seen the yellowing of his irises upon his return from Dublin, and recognized the silence that followed for days as he struggled to understand what he had done to the poor prostitute in the brothel. Now, there was no

Christy Lynn

denying both her children had fallen under the curse. Part of her rejoiced, for they would never know the embrace of death. But the other part of her mourned the life they would never know.

That night, hours into deep sleep, came the pounding at the door. When mother answered, the light from the torches spilled into the dark cottage. A small group of men took a step back when she came outside, wrapping a shawl around her shift in the name of modesty.

She shaded her tired eyes against the orange blaze. "Good eve' to ye, Mr. O'Byrne...Mr. MacBradaigh. How may I be of service at such an hour?" she asked politely, managing to look alarmed. "Is that ye over there, Mr. McCarthy? Whatever is the matter?"

"Pardon the intrusion, Mistress Whelan, we need a word with yer son," the man named O'Byrne spoke as the leader of the group.

Mother wrapped her shawl tighter around her thin frame, even though it was not a chilly night. "I might need to ask ye the nature of yer request." She eyed the pitchforks and clubs. "Ye appear as though yer set on an execution! Ye cannot expect a widowed mother to keenly hand her only son to a lot such as yerselves." She smiled in a flirtatious way to ease the sting of her remark, and the men laughed, shoulders relaxing and torches lowering as the tension of the intrusion eased a fraction.

Cailin Whelan was a known beauty and there

The Sacrifice

wasn't a man on the Isle of Ireland that could deny her, if she set her mind to have him. In fact, it was her beauty that prompted the wives of the local parish to whisper the rumor she was a witch. The sooner they were rid of Cailin Whelan, the better. She was too much of a threat to their marriage beds.

"McCarthy's boy, Colin, has yet to return home," O'Byrne explained, his voice less harsh than before. "He told his mother he was going hunting with yer son."

Cailin nodded slowly, as she gave the appearance of processing the situation. "Let me wake the lad, for 'tis all too true, he was hunting since dawn with young Colin."

Upon her admission to seeing Colin, the men seemed greatly relieved. She slipped back inside, closing the door quietly behind her. She faced her twins, managing not to look anxious for their sakes. She rushed to Barrex, taking both his hands in hers and staring straight into his eyes. "Ye hunted rabbits with Colin 'til the heat of the day, when ye thought to take a swim in the river. A couple of lasses...ye'll refuse to name them for their reputation's sake...had appeared with the same idea. As yer soon to propose marriage, ye left Colin to his own diversions, not wishing to be tempted by desire and wrong your true love."

She squeezed his hands tightly. "Do ye understand me, son? Ye've not seen him since, but ye have his share of the kills from this morning's hunt. Give the meat to Mr. McCarthy and ask if ye might help search for Colin, him being yer closest friend."

It was the twins' first lesson in deceit for the sake of survival.

***

Barrex carried out his mother's instructions precisely as they were given, and over the next week, the prominent men from the village began inviting him to dinners and on hunting expeditions in order to press him further for the names of the young girls he had supposedly left Colin to swim with in the river. Brigid and Cailin were obliged to receive several women from the parish, whom had never visited through the years they had lived in the county, accepting their vehement apologies they had not paid a call sooner. Of course, it was all a plot to attempt to learn information through any means necessary; even something as extreme as visiting the Whelan cottage.

Sunday evening, Barrex stumbled into the house, holding his ribs and spitting at the blood running into his mouth from his gushing nose! "Oh, my word!" Mother exclaimed. "What happened to ye?"

Barrex explained the McCarthy's were

The Sacrifice

starting to spread word through the village that Cailin was a witch and had sacrificed young Colin to Satan. Upon hearing such nonsense, Barrex challenged Colin's older brother to step outside of the pub they were in at the time. Unfortunately, Barrex's family pride was much keener than his ability to fight. The elder McCarthy son beat him to a pulp in the village square.

He slouched in a chair, unshed tears blurring his vision, aided by his broken nose. "Have ye nothing ye can do for it?" he pointed at the crooked appendage, wickedly out of joint beneath the blackening skin.

Mother shrugged. "Do not fuss over it, in another hour ye'll not even know it had ever been broken; such is yer immortal body's ability to heal itself."

Both Barrex and Brigid looked at her with surprised curiosity. "Of what do you speak, Mother?" Brigid asked.

"I have been teaching ye both of the curse in which ye have received, and with the curse come a few blessings. Ye're immortal, as I have said. Therefore, yer body has the power to heal itself faster than any human could imagine. Here, let me have a look at ye," Cailin stood behind Barrex and lightly pressed on the swollen bridge of his nose.

"Shite!" he yelled. "It hurts!"

"Ye'll get used to the pain, son. But we shan't

Christy Lynn

have it heal all crooked so ye go through eternity with a bent nose." Before Barrex could ask what she intended to do, Cailin snapped the joint cleanly in place, eliciting a sharp cry from her patient, but nothing further. "Better?"

Brigid fetched a basin of water and a cloth to clean the blood from her brother's face, then the three of them sat down to supper. "I've written a letter to Abbot Eoghan Doyle. He's to procure safe lodgings for ye both within the walls of Glenstal Abbey. My most beloved friend, Annaline Fainn, shall arrive tomorrow as support for myself when ye both depart. Ye'll not worry for me, she will stay until ye both are able to return home."

"What are ye saying, Mother? Ye'll not accompany us?" Brigid's face paled with panic.

She told them she would stay behind until the gossip and intrigue from the local parishioners settled, then she would write to them to return home where they could resume their lives safely. She had a plan; she would grace the church with her presence, something she had yet to do upon arriving seventeen years ago, slip into the confessional and cry her hardest to the priest. She would be sure to express her fervent desire to unburden her heart with the truth of the disappearance of Colin McCarthy.

She would tell the priest of Colin's seduction of her innocent daughter. How he only befriended Barrex in order to become close to Brigid. Then,

The Sacrifice

she would confess Brigid's moment of sinful weakness. Colin pledged his true love for her in the forest the night he disappeared, promising marriage. Brigid, so fresh and full of dreams of a handsome husband, gave herself willingly to him. However, Colin had not anticipated Barrex coming to look for his sister because the hour was late.

Upon discovering them both in a compromising position, Barrex threatened Colin with his life, but the boy was consumed with guilt for ruining Brigid's future prospects. Once he had, shall we say, relieved himself inside her, destroying her chances at a decent marriage in the future, he fled to Dublin where he could blend in unknown and not face the repercussions of his actions.

It took most of the evening, but mother was able to convince her children it was the right course of action. She had to see them safely away first, however, as they were simply too young to lose their newly inherited gifts of immortality to the burning pyres built by ignorant men.

CHAPTER 15

The next morning, Annaline Fainn appeared at the Whelan cottage. She fell into Cailin's arms in a kindred embrace, announcing that all would be fine, now that she was there. In truth, the situation did feel less grim with her positive energy and enthusiasm radiating throughout the cozy home. Brigid and Barrex were in awe of her, who was this woman?

"Cay, they are simply beautiful!" Annaline squealed when she saw Brigid and Barrex huddled together, looking like a pair of fawns ready to dash away from a predator.

"Thank ye," Cailin replied, beaming at her offspring. "They have grown so fast."

"And you say they have inherited the gift?" Annaline leaned against Cailin's shoulder with the same ease and comfort of a sister.

"There's no need to talk of us as if we are not here," Barrex said.

Cailin waved a long, slender hand at her twins, motioning for them to come closer. "Introduce yerselves to yer Auntie Anne. Do not act as if ye've no manners."

Brigid was enraptured! She had never seen a woman as lovely as her own mother, but this woman was enchanting in her own right. She was

The Sacrifice

fresh and so full of life, a constant reddish glow warmed her cheeks; the same red as her brilliant hair. Brigid instantly adored her.

"I'm your mother's oldest friend," explained Annaline. She was instantly bombarded by such questions as how long have ye known our mother? How ever did ye meet her?

It did not take long for Annaline to win their trust and love, and before mid-afternoon, the four of them were chattering and laughing through the daily chores. Brigid overheard her mother and new auntie expressing how wonderful it was to finally see each other again. She got the impression it had been years since their last reunion. Regardless of the unfortunate circumstances that caused Mother to send for Anne, Brigid was greatly relieved she had such a loyal friend by her side, if she and Barrex must seek refuge in the Abbey in County Limerick.

Barrex fell asleep before the sky had darkened fully to black, but the women sat up long after moonrise, talking quietly in the hushed haze of candlelight. "You are an incredible beauty, Brigid. You favor your mother." Anne smiled at Brigid, who was blushing under such praise.

"That one is the exact image of his father," Cailin nodded her head in the direction of Barrex's sleeping form.

Anne nodded in agreement. ""Tis the black hair, just like…"

Christy Lynn

"We do not speak of their father," Cailin interrupted Annaline, and Brigid's brow furrowed in concern. It was as if Mother was trying to keep Auntie Anne from saying something she shouldn't.

"We were born twelve hours apart," Brigid interjected. She wanted so badly to add to the conversation that she blurted whatever first came to mind.

Anne smiled kindly at her, tilting her head as though she were admiring a pretty little doll on a shelf. "I know, dear, I was there."

Brigid turned to her mother with wide eyes. "Is it true, Mother?"

"Aye, it is."

Brigid settled back into her chair and sipped her cup of tea in quiet contemplation. There was so much she did not know about her own mother...what other things were yet to be discovered? A small, stinging pain pinched her between her thighs, fading as quickly as it began, but it was an uncomfortable reminder of Colin McCarthy and that night in the woods that already seemed a lifetime ago.

"Brigid, might you explain to me exactly what took place with the McCarthy boy?"

The question startled Brigid from her thoughts, making her hand jerk and a wee amount of tea splash over the rim of the cup and drip on her skirt. Nervously, she looked to her mother,

The Sacrifice

silently asking permission to tell the story. Of course, Cailin gave her a nod to encourage her to answer Anne.

The details of the event were told, sparing nothing. She spoke of the liberties he instantly assumed he could take upon dragging her off the road. Being an honest sort, she admitted that she did not mind his assumptions, nor did she try to discourage him. "He felt...very good to touch," she admitted, feeling ashamed she took pleasure in what had happened.

Anne lifted a brow and grinned. "Indeed, he did. Now, will you tell of why you killed him?"

The words were spoken so bluntly, without the sugar coating Barrex and her mother were sure to use when discussing the topic. "Well...I-I mean to say...well," Brigid stammered. She was so embarrassed! It was difficult to explain, but she didn't want the magnificent Annaline Fainn to think she had committed such a horrendous crime. "I am not so certain it was I who took his life, Auntie."

Anne gave Cailin a confused look. "Is that so, Cay? Is there another party involved in the young man's demise?"

Cailin smiled apologetically and shook her head. "No. Brigid is yet to come to terms with her power."

"Ohh, I see." Anne returned her attention to Brigid. "Little dove, why did you kill that boy?"

Christy Lynn

she repeated the question.

Brigid's heart was hammering in her chest, but there was no denying her guilt, so she may as well own up to it. "I was angry!" she finally shouted. "I thought he loved me, Auntie Anne! He was so cruel. He said he was going to marry me, took my maidenhead, hurt me in the doing, then, dared to call me such names as a witch and the devil's own child. He did his bidding inside me." Her face blazed red. "Then said he must tell everyone what I was."

By Anne's posture, it was obvious she was intrigued. She was leaning forward in her chair, hands tightly clasped in her lap. "Go on, what did you do?"

"He was so weak. I know not why he became so, and he could barely walk. He was stumbling along the road, shouting and struggling to get away from me. I could not understand why. What had I done, other than please him? I began to realize he had used me as a whore." Upon speaking it allowed, her anger flashed again in her eyes. "If Colin McCarthy thought he was going to ruin my reputation after using me as such, he was wrong! I fell on top of him and kissed him - hard. I hated him then, and I bit his lips. When I tasted his blood I spit it back on his face. Auntie Anne, please believe me, I have no idea, even still, why I kissed him and he died."

The older women sat quietly for a moment,

The Sacrifice

and when Anne finally looked at Cailin with sympathy, Cailin shrugged dismissively. "Brigid, that young man said those hurtful words out of fear of your power over him. I want you to understand. "She touched Brigid's cheek tenderly.

"Yes, Auntie." Brigid felt like a small child again, not a young woman of sixteen.

"Good. Do not forget it. Tell me, after this Colin violated you, how did you feel?"

Brigid tucked her chin toward her chest. "I felt strong and so happy. I felt wonderful," she murmured into her small bosom.

Anne placed her index finger under Brigid's chin and made her raise her eyes to meet hers. She gave her a pleased smile. "You want to feel like that always, do you not?"

Brigid nodded, unsure if she should admit to such a wicked thing. "Yes, I do, but Colin is gone, so..."

"What does that have to do with it?" Anne quipped. "You may feel such life in your veins any time you wish."

"Annaline!" Cailin hissed at her friend. "She's too young to hear such truths."

"Nonsense, Cay! She is sixteen, and Colin was only the first of many. He opened her. Do you assume she will not couple again soon?"

Cailin's face paled slightly. By the expression on her face, it was obvious such a thought had not occurred to her. "I have spoken with Brigid and

Christy Lynn

she has assured me she has no desire to repeat the act until she is married."

"Oh, for the love of Lucifer!" Anne exclaimed, causing Brigid to cover her mouth in horror at such sacrilege. "Cay, have you lost your mind? I am certain young Brigid is sincere in her intentions, however, she is what she is. If you do not take care to instruct her," she paused to add emphasis to the next words. "May the Gods take pity on mankind."

***

It had taken considerable effort to get Brigid onto the Abbot's wagon, but the twin succubi were on their way to sanctuary, at last. They watched as the little cottage, shrouded in the deep shadows of the forest, disappeared quickly from view. Once the horses turned onto the main road, Brigid had the strangest feeling her life would never be the same again.

Visitors always brought significant energy to the abbey, and the arrival of the twins had monks and nuns, alike, in a frenzy to assure their young wards were adequately provided for. Their comfort was of the utmost importance. Barrex acclimated quite quickly to the pace of life within the stone walls, but Brigid had her guardian, Sister Mabyn, in a fit of anxiety. They had been at the abbey for four days and Brigid had yet to step

The Sacrifice

foot outside her small room.

Never one to be too proud, Barrex was happy to help with any task or chore that needed done, and on the fifth day since their arrival, Abbot Eoghan Doyle found him on his hands and knees in the nave scrubbing the stone floor with as much reverence as a parishioner in confession. Being of considerable age, Father Doyle found it difficult to join Barrex on the flagstones, but he managed to do so without alerting the boy of his presence. Not until the priest was neatly settled a foot behind him, did Barrex realize he had company.

"Father Doyle!" he laughed. "Ye startled me." Barrex gave the Abbot a warm smile as his gaze took notice of Father Doyle's robe. Even as a young lad, Barrex had been attracted to fashion – and men - even though he had not yet admitted the latter to himself. "That's a terribly nice garment to be wearing if ye intended upon helping me scrub a floor," he joked with his elder.

The Abbot smiled kindly and managed to look somewhat embarrassed by the fact he was wearing such an impressive article. He seemed to feel quite out of place, all of a sudden. "I would like nothing more than to take brush in hand and help ye, lad, but I've other matters to attend to this day." His Scottish accent rolled smoothly from his tongue. Father Doyle had a Scottish mother and Irish father. When his father was killed in battle when he was but a boy, his mother took him to

Christy Lynn

Scotland where her family could help raise him.

Barrex sensed perhaps the Abbot's visit was of a serious nature, and he should cease his humor at once. "Forgive me, Father, I did not mean to be rude."

Father Doyle's brows crunched together as he vehemently shook his head. "No, no, lad, I mean not to put a somber note on the day. I simply wanted to have a word with ye before a meeting requested of me by Sister Mabyn."

Upon mention of the sister's name, Barrex became suddenly concerned. He knew she was Brigid's chaperone during their stay, and the fact the sister was requesting a private audience with the Abbot eluded to perhaps a problem. Immediately, he sat back on his heels and wiped his hands dry on his tunic. Patiently, he waited for Father Doyle to begin.

It was true, what Brigid said about Abbot Eoghan Doyle; he was most definitely a fearsome looking creature. His eyebrows were so bushy, they looked as though they would benefit from the use of a comb! To accentuate his sharp features and deep-set, dark eyes, the brows grew naturally at a harsh angle that brought them straight down toward his nose. The effect, unfortunately, made the Abbot look as if he was in a constant state of rage.

Even though Barrex had discovered during his time thus far in the abbey that the Abbot was one

The Sacrifice

of the kindest men he had ever met thus far, it was easy to forget when seeing him sitting in quiet contemplation with those fierce-looking brows. Barrex could easily understand why Eoghan Doyle was a successful Abbot – he easily commanded the fear and respect of his parish, which seemed very important in this strange religion, and was able to do so simply from the way his God had created him.

It was settled, Barrex had officially developed his first crush on a man. True, Father Doyle was not considered handsome by most, but Barrex was attracted to the father figure he sensed deep inside the man. He'd never met his own father, and therefore, had a strong attraction to side, kind men of power. To Barrex, Father Eoghan Doyle was beautiful.

After what seemed a very long time, Father Doyle looked up from his hands, which were folded neatly in his lap. "I dare not pry in the private lives of others, dear boy," he began, his voice soft and pleasant enough to invite open, unguarded conversation. "So, if I ask a question too intrusive, ye only need tell me and I shall withdraw my inquiry."

It was Barrex's turn to crunch his eyebrows in concern. "No, Father, ye could not ask a question too personal." He leaned forward in keen interest, elated to have the Father's attention.

Father Doyle smiled, a broad smile that

Christy Lynn

carved several small divots in his full cheeks and managed to, dare one say, make him attractive, in a way. "Ye are too kind, lad. But what I wish to ask may shock ye. However, I regret I must ask. This...er...debacle between yer sister and that lad from yer village, was it, by chance, yer sister's first love?"

The question did shock Barrex, as the Father predicted it might, but he was relieved it was nothing more serious. Thoughtfully, he nodded. "Yes, to my knowledge, it was."

Father Doyle looked suddenly stricken with grief. His gaze dropped to his lap, once again, and he squeezed his eyes tightly closed, as if trying to escape an unimaginable pain.

"Are ye alright, Father?" Barrex placed his hand on the Abbot's forearm and tilted his head in order to better see the Abbot's face.

"Yes, my son, I am perfectly fine," Father Doyle opened his eyes, smiled sadly, and patted Barrex's hand where it rested questioningly on his arm. But Barrex noticed a change in the Father's posture as he did so.

Suddenly, a strange look crossed the Father's face, and Barrex saw him blink rapidly a few times, as if dismissing an odd feeling or thought. The Father rubbed his forehead, looking tired, whereas, only a moment ago he seemed quite motivated. "Forgive me, I did not sleep so well, and I fear it is catching up to me."

The Sacrifice

Barrex, on the other hand, felt instantly refreshed. He had unknowingly swiped a little of the Father's chi and was in the midst of confusing the exchange of energy with the makings of true love. "Well, if I may ever be of service, Father...," he smiled broadly, the invitation meaning more than the words eluded to.

Mother had never warned the twins that the act of sex, itself, was not the only way to pilfer chi from a human. They had no idea that simple contact would affect those around them.

Father Doyle, never suspecting the hidden invitation behind the young man's offer, squeezed Barrex's shoulder in a paternal way and patted his cheek. "Ye are a most kind-hearted lad. Thank ye, I shall be sure to rely upon ye, if I have need."

He gathered his feet beneath him and began the struggle to stand. Barrex hopped up and offered his hand to help his senior off the cold, hard floor. Father Doyle straightened his heavy robes and rubbed the back of his neck, sighing as he did so. "Barrex, ye know yer sister better than any among us. Perhaps, is there anything at all ye can think of that might assist her in her time of grief?"

It was then that Barrex suddenly realized he had not seen Brigid in two days! The last time he laid eyes on her was when he went to visit her in her room. She had looked disheveled and her eyes were puffy from crying. He assumed she was

Christy Lynn

distraught over leaving their home and their mother, which no doubt played a part in her depression, but he had never thought about the possibility she was mourning Colin.

His heart broke for her in that moment. To think, not only had she lost her first love, but she was also dealing with the truth that her loss was of her own doing. How could he be so insensitive to his sister at a time like this?

"No, Father, I cannot think what might bring cheer to her in this moment," he finally answered. "I must go to her."

Father Doyle held up his hand to stop Barrex in his haste. "Yes, son, ye must, but not straight away. Please, allow me to speak with her first?"

Of course, the Abbot was the head of Glenstal Abbey, his word was law. So, to ask permission from a visitor if he may speak to another under his roof was only polite. He would do as he wished. Knowing this, Barrex begrudgingly consented. He would go to Brigid later, after the last meal of the day.

The Sacrifice

CHAPTER 16

Father Doyle was pleased to find Brigid in the courtyard, sitting silently on a stone bench with her head bent, as if in prayer. As he approached, he saw she was holding a rosary in her slender fingers and seemed to be staring most fascinated at the small beads. Quietly, he took a seat next to her and inhaled a deep, purifying breath.

"I love the smell of the flowers in this garden. The sisters are miraculous in their abilities with the roses." He gave Brigid the same smile Barrex found so disarming.

Brigid wasn't looking at the Abbot though; her gaze intent on the rosary in her hands, and she continued twirling one of the small, black beads between her forefinger and thumb. "Yer God must love his people very much," she whispered, although her mind was as far from the Lord as it could be. She couldn't remove the recollection of Colin's hands on her body, which made her guilt over killing him that much more severe. She murdered the young man, how dare she take pleasure in their love making beforehand!

One of the Abbot's bushy eyebrows rose in surprise. "Why, yes! Yes, he does. But what is it that enlightened ye to the love of Christ?"

Christy Lynn

Brigid was terrified of Father Doyle, but his voice, as he spoke to her this moment, was so kind and tender. She felt it was safe to speak her thoughts. "I was not speaking of the love of the Christ. See, none of our Gods would dream of protecting and loving those who tortured and killed His only son. Sister Mabyn told me of the sacrifice God allowed His son to make for the redemption of mankind. Now they may enter the Heaven that was originally created for them to begin with."

Father Doyle tried to hide his smile at her innocent comparison of her pagan gods to the Anglo-Saxon God. "Perhaps they would not. I cannot say for certain. I must confess I am not well educated in the belief in which ye and Barrex were raised." He stretched his legs out in front of him, his robes so long as to only allow the tips of his shoes to show from beneath the hemline. Brigid suddenly giggled, thinking he looked like a wizard from a bedtime story.

"Ye laugh at my shoes?" Father Doyle laughed with her, tapping the toes of the battered sandals together.

"No!" she protested, the giggling turning into a deep belly laugh. It wasn't that funny, but the healing power of joy was desperately needed, and her body knew it. So, she let the laughter come as it may.

When they both settled again, the atmosphere

The Sacrifice

felt more comfortable and Brigid dared to look at the Abbot's face. Immediately, she regretted it; he was still as frightening as before. Quickly, she fixed her gaze back on his shoes.

They sat silently for some time, just listening to the bees buzzing among the vegetation of the courtyard. Finally, Father Doyle broke the silence. "I am happy to see ye smile."

Brigid smiled again, for his sake, but it lacked sincerity. Her attention remained focused on the plain rosary. "If I pray for the soul of a lost loved one, using these beads, Sister Mabyn says he may enter Heaven, even though he had wronged me."

"'Tis a very kind act to pray for another's entrance into Heaven and out of Purgatory. God will be most pleased with ye. Especially, if ye pray for the soul of a person who has wronged ye." He didn't want her to know he was aware of what took place between her and the McCarthy boy. Father Doyle didn't know the entire truth, however, and was under the hope that Colin would return to his family soon enough.

"Have you eaten breakfast?" he continued. He saw her nod, but she offered no interest in a conversation. Still, it was his duty to try to help those suffering. "I have been in close communication with the McCarthy lad's father. I will be certain to inform ye the moment they discover his whereabouts. I am sure he will turn up in a day or two." He took Brigid's hand that was worrying the little beads and gave it a sturdy squeeze.

"Ye think him alive, Father?"

Without hesitation Father Doyle answered, "yes, I do. Do not doubt it. Ye would not know it to look at me now, but I was a young man once, as well, and I was known to sneak off in the middle of the night from my parent's home to seek the diversions of town." The revelation that an Abbot could be so human startled Brigid and she looked at him with wide, incredulous eyes. "My word, child, is it truly that hard to imagine I was once young?" he chuckled.

Brigid hastily composed herself, feeling terrible for offending the old man. "No, father, it is not. I apologize, truly. It was a shock, perhaps, to hear ye ran away from home to go to a town. May I confess, I have had the same thoughts."

"Of course, ye have, my dear. But young lasses are much wiser than young lads, and ye would never attempt to ruin yer reputation in such a way."

Father Doyle was only teasing, but it was instantly clear he had said the wrong thing, somehow. Brigid's face fell, her eyes looking suddenly haunted. He literally saw her withdrawing back inside the protective shell in which she had been residing since her arrival. He regretted whatever it was he had said to cause her lovely smile to fade.

The Sacrifice

The mention of a ruined reputation caused the events of that evening with Colin behind the oak tree to come rushing back with full force. Embarrassed, she turned away to discreetly wipe a tear from her lashes.

"Ye know, lass," the Abbot began in his thick, Scottish accent. "Yer heart will never feel a pain quite as sharp as your first heartbreak. No man shall be able to hurt ye again in quite the same way." Father Doyle had obviously never had a daughter of his own, but in that moment, he knew the fury a father feels when his daughter is hurt by a man. He wanted to go find this Colin McCarthy and beat him to a pulp for making such a lovely, innocent girl cry.

Slowly, Brigid turned to face the Abbot. His kind words had made her speechless and she suddenly saw him in a different light. In a moment of gratitude, she flung herself at him and gave him a sincere hug, nearly knocking him off the bench. Knowing she needed to express herself in such a way, Father Doyle allowed the embrace. As he held her in return, he saw Sister Mabyn smiling through tears as she stood, concealed, under a thick arbor of vines.

***

Father Doyle's talk had worked magic on Brigid's mood, and by late afternoon, she had managed to

Christy Lynn

wash her face and don a clean dress for dinner. As she strolled toward the kitchen with Sister Mabyn, chatting idly of herbs and their medicinal uses, Barrex suddenly appeared, sweaty and out of breath from running.

Without a word, he swooped his sister up in his arms and just held her a moment before whispering in her ear, "I'm so sorry, Blue! I'm so sorry!"

"What are ye speaking of, Barry?"

Barrex just shook his head, at a loss for words how to tell Brigid he never meant to be so insensitive to what she was going through. She looked different, somehow; older. The yellowing of her green eyes gave her a fearsome beauty; beauty that would ensure her survival in the centuries to follow.

He walked with the women to the dining hall, passively chatting about the work that had been keeping him busy these five days. Brigid felt selfish; having never left her rooms had made her exempt from otherwise hard labor. She was by no means lazy, and her face began to heat from the embarrassment of not offering her services to the nuns – when there was obviously so much that needed done.

Just as they were approaching the large room, with its delicious aromas wafting toward them on a light breeze, one of the sisters Brigid had not seen before hurried toward them. She explained

The Sacrifice

they must follow her to Father Doyle's chambers at once!

Brigid, cross from her plans of a hot meal being so abruptly thwarted, was suddenly overjoyed to see Auntie Annaline standing near the fire in the Abbot's dark room. "Auntie Anne, how good it is to see ye!" She fell into Anne's waiting embrace. "Have ye come to take us home?"

When Brigid pulled back to look at her, she saw not the fresh, vibrant woman who had appeared only days ago on their doorstep. This woman was drained of happiness, dark smudges under her eyes, and her appearance a frightful mess. "Whatever is the matter, Auntie?"

Annaline took her by the hand and led her to a chair. She gratefully accepted a small glass of wine from the Abbot, and Brigid shivered with dread when a glass was also offered to her and her brother - along with a grim, sympathetic look on the Abbot's face.

"I bring most terrible news," Anne began. "A mob...," her voice broke suddenly, and she sipped her wine slowly to hide the sob escaping her throat. "The villagers came looking for you, Barrex." She shook her head and squeezed her eyes closed.

Brigid felt as if she were dreaming. The room looked suddenly blurry and she couldn't understand what Anne was trying to tell them.

Christy Lynn

Why was Barrex hanging his head, his shoulders shaking slightly? "What are ye saying, Auntie? Say it plainly, I implore ye."

"Listen, little doves, I must tell you something most tragic." She turned toward the Abbot, who Barrex was busy ogling. "Father, forgive me for what I must say...and for what had to be done." She made the sign of the Christian cross over her bosom, then faced the twins again. "Your mother, she made me promise if the worst was to happen, I would not let her burn at the stake."

Brigid covered her mouth in horror. "What are ye saying? Where is Mother?"

Anne reached for her hand and squeezed it. "The time had come the villagers would hear no more excuses. They wanted blood for that McCarthy boy. It took them only a moment to turn the blame from you, Barrex, to your mother when they discovered the two of you had been taken to safety and was beyond their reach. They said your mother was to burn for bewitching her children and sacrificing the McCarthy boy to Satan."

"Holy Mother of God," the Abbot murmured, sliding silently into a chair, his eyes wide with distress and pity.

"Your mother made me promise, you see! I never thought I would have to make good on such an oath, but as always, she was right. She knew what would come to pass. So, as the shouts for

The Sacrifice

justice in the dooryard grew louder, I hurriedly mixed the concoction that would allow Cailin to slip into an...an eternal sleep," Anne paused to swallow the lump in her throat. "By the time they tied her to the post in the square, she was unconscious. I swear upon my honor, she felt no pain."

Brigid stared at her, mouth opened slightly in disbelief. "Are ye saying...? No, it cannot be," she whispered.

They wept, there in the dark room of the Abbot's private chamber, well into the night. Annaline revealed the last wishes of their mother, once they were able to listen, and it was decided the twins would go to London to live with her. Brigid never forgave Anne for her part in her mother's demise, and they never saw their childhood cottage in the forest again. Regardless, how often Barrex tried to reason with Brigid that Annaline had no choice but to make the poison that ended their mother's life, or else their mother would have suffered unimaginable pain in the flames of the pyre, Brigid turned a deaf ear. She vowed she would one day repay Anne for her so-called mercy.

CHAPTER 17

The elevator doors opened to the Tower penthouse, and Brigid bolted into the foyer like a caged animal just released into the wild. "Where are they, Anne?" she asked, trying to keep the hostility from seeping into her tone. She needed Anne to remain in that place of soft reverie in hopes of playing on her feelings to negotiate for Den's life.

Anne tossed her head. "In the sitting room, of course."

She suddenly grabbed Brigid by the elbow. "Listen to me. Take your brother and go. You cannot be here when Lilith arrives! It is by her command no one must witness her presence. It's most vital."

Brigid was momentarily caught in confusion by Anne's sincerity. She knew Anne better than anyone, and Anne seemed genuinely concerned for their safety. They had shared vast ages together, perhaps there was some remnant of a heart still left in that petrified chest.

"You know I can't do that, Anne. I...," she paused, glancing in the direction of the sitting room. She decided right then to try to appeal to Anne's love for her. She took Anne's hand tightly in her own. "I love him," she whispered, not

The Sacrifice

wanting anyone else to hear.

Anne nodded slowly, inhaling a deep breath. "I know you do."

Discovering that Anne already knew of her true feelings for Den, but was still determined to give him to Lilith, pissed Brigid off royally! She yanked her hand from Anne's grasp and made a point to wipe her palm on her pants, as if to imply she was contaminated by Anne's touch. Anne rolled her eyes and shoved Brigid toward the sitting room.

The penthouse had been miraculously transformed! The living room was aglow with a hundred candles, the glass wall was covered, blocking the stunning view of Manhattan at night, and all the furniture had been removed. An altar, of sorts, was constructed in the center of the space. It consisted of an elevated, platform bed, several feet high. Lush linens and furs were piled on top of the feather-stuffed mattress, along with tons of pillows. Incents perfumed the room and classical guitar played softly in the background. The stage was set, so to speak, for a night of romance.

It took a moment for Brigid to realize Den was tied up and laying on the altar; the perfect lamb to slaughter. Quickly, she ran to the bed and jumped on top of him. "I'm so sorry, I tried to keep this from happening," she cried into his ear.

"It's alright, it's alright, shush," Den's voice

had that soothing quality she needed, but it wasn't helping this time.

She buried her face in his chest; his smell filling her nose. Small dabs of tears smeared his skin, making Brigid want to put a shirt on him. He was hers, no matter what Anne said, and she didn't want him on display like this.

As soon as Brigid was able to catch her breath again from seeing him bound on an altar, waiting for a goddess to arrive and murder him, she became worried about his well-being. Quickly, she inspected his body, interrogating him over ever little bruise or cut she could find. His hands were restrained in front of him on his stomach, which is Anne's favorite way to bind a person, and Brigid caught a glimpse of red streaked across the backside of his right hand. "What happened?" she exclaimed.

Den grinned, seemingly pleased by her concern of him. "Let's just say I didn't go willingly. That Murphey guy is no easy foe." He turned his head and glared at Marshall Murphey.

She climbed off the platform and gave Mr. Murphey a look that would disintegrate stone! Her fists rested on her hips and her jaw muscles flexed as she ground her teeth. "It wasn't enough to abduct a human being against their will, but you had to rough him up in the process?"

Marshall's eyes flew open wide in surprise. "What? Was I supposed to just stand there and let

The Sacrifice

him pound on me? If that's what you're thinking, then think again." He turned his back to her and pretended to be busy reading something on his phone.

Brigid suddenly turned to Anne, her face brightening from a thought that just popped in her head. "He hasn't told you, has he?" she smiled, coyly.

Anne put her hands on her hips and frowned. "I admire your grit, Brig, you don't give up easily. You never have. It won't make a difference but go ahead and tell me."

"We think he's an Incubus," she stated flatly. Brigid watched as a glimmer of shock flashed behind Anne's eyes, but disappeared just as quickly.

"Right," she smiled patronizingly.

"You even said he was a powerhouse of chi! I've spent the past several days with him, and our souls are bound. Believe me, he's an Incubus." Brigid glanced at Den, her heart beating wildly from his close proximity. She simply wanted this over so they could hide away from the world and just be together. "Anne, you know me. could I be this in love with a human? He is my intended, my betrothed by the Gods. Only a succubus who has finally found her incubus mate..."

"Enough talk!" Anne yelled. Struggling to maintain her composure, she patted her hair and paused, taking a deep breath. "I'm sorry, little dove, but a sacrifice is to be made tonight, and it's going to take place; no matter what."

"So, you think the Goddess won't realize what he is the moment she kisses him?" Barrex interjected. "And where do you think she'll aim her wrath? It is said that if Lilith draws the life from one of her children, she, too, shall die." His eyes suddenly lit with an epiphany. "Is that your plan? Has that been the plan all along? You're attempting to kill the Lilith in order to gain control over us all, aren't you?"

"Enough!" Anne screamed. Marshal Murphy stepped closer to her side, his hand reaching suggestively toward his firearm. "Take them to my bedroom but leave the sacrifice where he is. Enough of this bullshit! It's nearly midnight. Its time."

Barrex was, of course, only trying to muddy the waters, so to speak. He knew Anne would never dream of such a plot. She was too much a coward to take on the Goddess; as were all succubi. Lilith reigned supreme - their loving creator - and would for eternity.

Marshal grabbed Brigid and cuffed her hands behind her back, exerting his physical power as she struggled against him. "Be still!" he hissed into her hair, pulling her against his chest and ushering her toward the bedroom.

"Anne, please, let me stay with Den! Aaanne!" Brigid begged, but Marshal pushed her into the

The Sacrifice

other room and slammed the door shut.

A few moments later, Barrex was tossed in the room with her. Brigid felt a tremor run through the thick carpeting, it was as if the entire building shivered from a chill. "She's here," she said, looking at her brother with real fear. "Will she kill him when she finds him to be an incubus?"

Barrex shook his head. "I don't know, Blue. I would imagine she isn't going to be very happy about it. But I'd think Anne is the one in danger for her choosing him. It's her responsibility to interview and qualify a proper sacrifice. And if Lilith is somehow damaged during the ordeal, Anne will probably die tonight."

Just then, Brigid heard a commotion on the other side of the door. She couldn't stand it! Her soul mate, an incubus who could love her and live by her side through the ages, was in peril and she could no longer stand by and do nothing. "Barry, help! Get these off me," she whispered.

Barrex's hands were tied in front of him, as well, so he had little trouble swiping a bobby pin from the dresser. He fumbled with the small lock in the cuffs around his sister's wrists. It didn't help that Brigid was wiggling around in her desperation to get to Den in time.

"Hold still," he reprimanded. "Is Den really an incubus?"

"Yes," she answered bluntly.

"Well, at least you had the good sense to fall in

love with an immortal. Wish I could have been so fortunate."

Brigid stopped her squirming long enough to realize that her love for Den would change things between her and her twin brother. It had always been just the two of them, protecting each other always. What must it be like for Barrex to see her happily in love, after the agony he suffered for loving a man susceptible to death?

Finally, the steel shackles popped open and Brigid hurriedly untied her brother. She was first to burst into the room and what she saw turned her vision red. Anne was straddling Den, her face buried in his neck! She swiftly sat up, startled to see Brigid standing there. For once, Anne had nothing to say. Perhaps it was the look of lost sanity in Brigid's eyes, but Anne wisely said nothing at all.

The Goddess Lilith was nowhere to be seen, but the atmosphere in the penthouse was noticeably different. The air was charged, alive; like the beach during a lightning storm. One could almost smell the ozone. However, Brigid paid little heed; her man was being touched by another succubus and her jealousy was fully roused. "Blue," Barrex spoke, his voice dripping with reason. "Tread lightly, I know you're angry...,"

His words landed on deaf ears. She didn't even glance in his direction as he spoke to her. Her temper and focus was all on Anne. "What do

The Sacrifice

you think you're doing?" Brigid's nostrils flared.

Anne smiled her wicked smile, the one that never reaches her eyes and makes her look cold and ruthless. "I was only having a little fun. Jesus, lighten up, Brig." She turned her attention toward Den, who was still nestled between her thighs as she sat on him. "Brigid wasn't always such a tight ass, ya know? Used to be a really fun."

Brigid suddenly lunged for Anne! She threw her entire body weight into the assault and both women went tumbling to the floor. Several candles positioned on the floor around the altar were knocked over, but fortunately, the melted pools of wax around the lit wicks snuffed the singular flames before they were able to ignite and catch the place on fire. She grabbed Anne by the throat, reveling in the satisfying feeling of holding her life in her hands - literally.

All the suppressed anger due to the loss of her mother came spilling forth, and her hold on that fragile area of arteries and bones tightened. The wrath she had nursed all these years was now a fury fed by the fear of losing her one true love, and the combination was lethal. A small, wheeze escaped Anne's throat, and Brigid felt the muscles of her esophagus spasm under her palms.

She watched as Anne's face darkened to the frightening shade of a plum. Anne slapped at Brigid's wrists in attempt to break her hold, but it was useless; satisfaction and revenge was too

Christy Lynn

near; Brigid wasn't about to cheat herself of its sweetness.

Slowly, Brigid lowered her face to Anne's, hovering just inches above. It seemed everything was clearer, sharper in this moment. She noticed how Anne's lips were swelling from the pressure of trapped blood from Brigid's grasp. Lovingly, softly, she gave Anne a kiss on the lips and in the same instant, began shaking her violently! "Damn you, Annaline Fainn!" she growled between clenched teeth.

Suddenly, Brigid sealed her mouth over Anne's and began to suck the life out of her! Anne's arms flailed, thrashing madly in a ditch effort to stay alive. Brigid drew Anne's life from her with all the strength of all the hatred, pain, and love she felt for the woman beneath her. this was, perhaps the hardest thing she had ever done. Anne was like family. She felt Anne's pulse hammering against her palms, felt it begin to wane as her chi escaped her body and flowed through Brigid's veins.

"STOP!" A voice as sharp as a trumpet suddenly blasted through the air, scaring the shit out of everyone in the room!

Being completely consumed by the attempted murder of the Head Succubus, no one even noticed the timely arrival of the Goddess Lilith, herself. Everyone was suddenly eerily still; it seemed the room was frozen in time. Brigid stared,

The Sacrifice

eyes bulging at the sight of the Creator of all Succubi and Incubi.

What she saw caused her to lose her breath - and nearly her mind! Frantic, she searched the candlelit room for her brother. He was standing close by the altar, staring in disbelief at the vision before him. She watched him sink slowly to the floor, helpless to do anything else.

"Unhand her, Brigid. She's your sister!" the Goddess commanded.

Brigid felt Anne's long, thin neck slide from her grasp, but she couldn't tear her eyes away from Lilith. She heard Anne choking on the influx of fresh oxygen and felt her body stirring beneath hers.

Clumsily, she climbed from the altar and joined her twin on the floor. Barrex wrapped his arms around Brigid, holding her as if the end of the world was upon them, at last. He opened his mouth to speak, but no words came. It was Brigid who finally spoke, her lips numb from the shock. Her tone was filled with utter disbelief...

"Mother?"

Christy Lynn

The Sacrifice

Christy Lynn

THANK YOU

I would like to take this opportunity to thank you for reading The Sacrifice.

If you would like to find out more about me and my books, you can do so by visiting the following links:

Facebook
www.facebook.com/Authorchristylynn

Instagram
www.instagram.com/authorchristylynn

Book Formatting & Cover Design
sylv.net